*L*AURA, may I speak to you for a minute?"

Taking her arm, I steered my way among the other guests and led her to the center of the room. "Are you sure they're all blind?" I whispered.

She looked frankly astonished. "Of course I'm sure. This is a club of sorts, a very pleasant one, I might add, but its rules are quite strict: everyone except you is blind."

"Okay. Just imagine that they're all surrounding us at this very minute. Can you visualize that?"

"What are you driving at?" she asked, a trace of anxiety in her voice.

"You'll see."

I took her glass, carefully placed it on the floor, and drew her close to me. With my right hand I pulled down the zipper of her dress and caressed her back. Then I kissed her violently. . . .

# BLIND
# LOVE

a novel by

## *Patrick Cauvin*

A FAWCETT CREST BOOK • NEW YORK

*BLIND LOVE*

THIS BOOK CONTAINS THE COMPLETE TEXT OF THE
ORIGINAL HARDCOVER EDITION.

Published by Fawcett Crest Books, CBS Publications, the
Consumer Publishing Division of CBS Inc., by arrangement
with Houghton Mifflin Company

ISBN: 0-449-23483-5

Printed in Canada

10   9   8   7   6   5   4   3   2   1

# BLIND
# LOVE

# Neptune

*B*ERNIER!

I turned around. Briette—the students call her Bri-Bri—was running in the sunlight. The reflection of the sun on the school windows was so dazzling I couldn't see her clearly.

"What's up?"

Boys and girls crowded the schoolyard where I waited for her. The athletic type, she galloped toward me, sprinting like a girl scout, elbows hugging her sides.

Briette is my colleague in the department of natural sciences. I've known her for fourteen years. On weekends she looks after adolescents in pleated skirts and knee socks, dragging them off to the sparse woods that circle Paris. Sometimes I run into her at the Gare St. Lazare. Always in Bermuda shorts, a pack on her back, she strides back and forth like an Amazon, waiting for her charges. Her wholesome energy terrifies me.

Partial to shock methods, she is involved passionately—if I may put it that way—in the teaching of sex education. Her cupboard is crammed with gigantic posters. Some depict genital organs; others show men and women with transparent bellies and bemused expressions. All of them are replete with indicator arrows and scientific terminology.

One time last year, when we were standing on the staircase surrounded by students, she unrolled a really breathtaking poster. Brandishing the colored diagram like a standard, chin thrust forward, she looked for all the world like Napoleon on the bridge at Arcola.

"What do you think of it, pedagogically speaking?"

My forehead covered with sweat, I fled before the sound of her voice died away in the ancient corridors, thoroughly ashamed of possessing all that complicated plumbing, those lymphatic glands, that tangle of veins. I couldn't believe my insides were so intricate! The fifth graders looked at me disapprovingly—or so I thought. I wanted to tell them that I wasn't really built like that, that the scale of the drawing was exaggerated, but I knew it would be no excuse.

Anyway, this day, June 28, was the last day of the school year, the day for the distribution of prizes, for speeches and the inevitable school play.

Jacqueline Briette ground to a halt before me. Round glasses like headlights and large square teeth, reminding you of the front of a fifties Cadillac. I like her a lot.

She tossed me the news like a ball. "I've got my transfer for next year!"

Her transfer. She'd been dreaming of it for years. A native of the Haute-Garonne, the poor thing had been trying to get back there ever since the end of the war. But there was always some teacher with more diplomas who got the job. Cooped up in this Parisian hole, she looked older and older at the start of each year.

I didn't like the idea of her leaving. I don't like to leave people, either. I guess I'm funny that way, just an old prof. I like to return to my office year after year, and if they paint walls or change desks or faces, I'm unhappy —a hopeless stick-in-the-mud.

Not that I was ever a close friend of Briette's. She's much too athletic for me. Her volley-ball, camp-fire personality irritates me, but having had her around for so long I've become accustomed to the sound of her steps and her grating voice that sometimes pierces the wall of our adjoining classrooms. Without her, something will be missing.

"I'm happy for your sake."

We entered the hall together. I was wearing a tie as I did every year for this odious ritual. And I was hot. I'd have to buy a light suit, the kind they're wearing these days. Maybe a linen suit, like the one Versin, a graduating senior, had on. Except that he's only eighteen, has curly hair and is built like a cowboy. It wouldn't be right for me. I might as well buy a yo-yo while I'm at it. Not that I'm trying to look younger.

In any case, my shirt was sticking to my shoulder blades. It seemed that it was going to be an exceptionally hot summer. Even the shaded hall was scorching. Although the curtains had been drawn over the bay windows, the sun shone through. Some of my colleagues were already seated on folding chairs by the time I mounted the stage. More than two hours of being bored stiff listening to the principal repeat last year's speech which was the same as the year before. It was going to be rough! Well, I should be used to it by now.

"Good morning, Monsieur Bernier."

"Good morning." Old Madame Rebolot who teaches the natural sciences . . . She was wearing a floral print, a riot of colors, with a butterfly over the left breast, wild roses over the right, lavender heather here and there— the whole of it enveloping two hundred pounds. Close to retirement, soon she too would be gone. Perhaps this was her last year to distribute the prizes.

I sat down beside Briette in the second row, next to the potted palms. Funny thing about those plants, you see them only on graduation day; they die as soon as the ceremony is over.

"Well, my dear Bernier, are you looking forward to your holiday?"

That was Meunier—history and geography. He's quite a personality, the life of any party, the practical jokester of the school lunchroom. For years he's been hiding my napkin ring on an average of twice a week. We're all jokers in the teaching profession.

The pupils entered. In the back, groups of parents, dressed in their Sunday best, were milling around, hugging the door and blocking it. Why didn't they come forward? Too shy to enter this cultural sanctuary? Were they afraid that someone might offer them hashish or quiz them about Mao Tse-tung? . . .

The sound of voices rose. Two hundred people sat up in front of us, the latest arrivals filling the first rows. God, what heat! Thank heaven tomorrow I'll be in . . . it's hard to say exactly where, with all the holiday rush, so many leaving. If only that rotten battery holds up! No joke to get stuck on the autoroute. Maybe I shouldn't have accepted Anne's invitation, but we see so little of each other these days. I simply couldn't refuse. It might have hurt her feelings.

"Ladies and gentlemen, quiet, if you please . . ."

Carnot was shouting himself hoarse. It's no fun being vice principal, especially if your passion is fishing for trout and collecting stamps. Every time I'm invited to his house we go through the same ritual. Before the meal I admire his rods, reels, spoons and artificial flies. After coffee I rave about his uncanceled one-franc New Guinea vermilion, the jewel of his entire collection. Needless to say, I know absolutely nothing about fishing or stamp collecting, but I'm fond of Carnot. He's almost a friend.

Briette leaned toward me. "Where are you going this summer?"

My shirt came unstuck when I moved. I felt the sweat running down my ribs. "To the Midi above Menton."

"To visit friends?"

"Yes."

I've never alluded to Anne here. No one on the faculty knows about my marriage. But I did tell Carnot in confidence one evening. And the school board knows it too. I had to record it when I filled out the forms. Family status: divorced, one child.

"Quiet, please!"

Duverrier, the principal, ascended the stage, which by this time was well-filled. The entire faculty was on hand, all the teachers, well turned out, damp but smiling. No wonder we were smiling—it was finally over, we were about to take off. Two months in the country, two months without having to struggle each day—a ten-round battle, one against thirty. We were exhausted and delighted.

Slowly the noise subsided, a sea receding with the tide. Duverrier raised both arms like an orchestra conductor.

"If you please, if you please . . ."

Silence reigned. Duverrier enjoyed his power to calm the seething ocean from his vantage point on the cliff, this stage. Once a year Duverrier played Neptune.

A chuckle on the right, the noise of feet scraping, then a hush. He'd done it again!

Total stillness.

Suddenly something behind me exploded. I jumped as if catapulted from my chair. The *Marseillaise*! It happens every year but I always forget. The blare of the loudspeaker hidden behind the palms a few feet away almost broke my left eardrum. Stoically, I made the best of it, squeezed against Briette, who was beating time with her flat heels.

It was over! One final blast of the cymbals buzzed in my head as we resumed our seats. Next year I'm going to make damn sure I know where they put the loudspeaker and give it a wide berth. Also, I'd better tell the technician to lower the volume of the record player or one of these days he'll blow all the fuses.

In front of me the swelling ocean had subsided, the waves were gone. Neptune had the floor.

"Once again, I am gratified to say, we have gathered together here—parents, pupils, teachers, members of the staff—for this little ceremony that not one of us feels is antiquated or without purpose, but which for me . . ."

Never before had I noticed the vast amount of hair growing out of the bursar's ears, like masses of seaweed. My knees touched his chair and I could count the hairs on his neck. But what fascinated me was his ears. How could any sound penetrate that forest? Luckily I had no scissors with me, the temptation would have been hard to resist.

". . . And to whom do we owe such results? To you, the parents, who have helped us, whose support and constant vigilance aided us during the past year. Without you all our discipline, all our instruction, might well have been in vain. Your role, therefore . . ."

My hands were damp. I caught sight of Chétrier's profile at the other end of the hall. He's a teaching assistant in physics and chemistry. He was chewing gum, and as he leaned forward I could see his jaws move up and down. It would be funny if a student got up and said: "Chétrier, leave the room. And deposit your gum in the basket on your way out." That's the kind of thing you always hope for, but it never happens. More's the pity. What this show needs is a little diversion.

Madame Rebolot wiped her neck daintily with a heavily perfumed turquoise handkerchief, evoking visions of voluptuous women on scarlet sofas.

"And if, in spite of the turbulence in the world today, if, despite the upheavals of a universe that no longer offers young minds the kind of moral enrichment a wise person

might wish for, if, despite the violence, fear, and collapse
of certain values . . ."

Twenty-seven minutes. Neptune was breaking a record.
He always said the same thing, but each year it took him
longer. Maybe that's what happens when you get older.

Anyway, if all goes well, tomorrow at this time I'll be
in Lyon. That damn battery! Well, let's forget about it. I'll
be zooming along at ninety kilometers an hour when
suddenly a female hitchhiker will appear at a curve in
the road . . .

She signals and I brake. "Where are you going?"

"Menton."

She has a lovely voice, like a stream trickling over clean
gravel.

"Get in." Charming legs. She looks like Ursula Andress
but is even more attractive—if that's possible.

Second episode. My hands caress her golden hair. We're
on a deserted beach, the sand is hot and I look like Gary
Cooper at twenty-five. "Do you love me, Ursula?"

"Yes, Gary." We kiss . . .

I jumped at the loud storm of applause and frantically
clapped my damp palms. Bravo Neptune, well said. Too
bad he finished just when my dream was getting interesting. I was thirsty.

"Do you have time for a drink, Bernier?" Briette
whispered.

She wanted to offer me one for the road.

"Sure."

We'll all go to Marcel's, the café on the corner. I'll
order a Ricard with lots of water, a whole pitcher. I could
see it, smell it . . .

The prizes were being distributed. Neptune shook
hands with the winners. Blacherie read out their names
and their class teacher handed out the books.

"Chapoteau, Viviane!" I glimpsed the top of Viviane
Chapoteau's head, a small red chignon that wavered in

front of Duverrier, trembled in front of Blacherie, stopped in front of her prof and vanished.

"Evrard, Philippe!" He's very tall, I could see him above the others. It's always the same, they begin with the ten-year-olds and it goes on forever. My students would be last. Patience!

"Devinard, Nathalie!" I wondered how things would be at Anne's. She didn't say anything about the house in her letter, just that she was expecting me, she and Frédéric.

"Villeneuve, Françoise!" Maybe they were right not to get married, I really don't know. At any rate, it doesn't bother me that Anne is living with him. Sometimes I'm amazed at myself: maybe I'm not such a stuffed shirt after all. He bought that house in the village, or rather his parents paid for it. Fifty years ago Frédéric would have been a good match. Today he's a guy in blue jeans who is taking forever to get his degree in philosophy, who tans himself in the sun of the Alpes-Maritimes and sleeps with my daughter—and all of it with a serenity induced by Zen Buddhism, which he discussed endlessly in that café near the Place de la République when I met him for the first time. I'd rather see him with Anne than alone. He has a smile when he looks at her that takes me by surprise every time. Only at her does he smile that way.

Here we go, it was my turn to hand out prizes to members of my class. "Pardon me, pardon me . . ." I moved down the row, stepping on as few feet as possible and wondering if I'd be able to make myself heard above this infernal racket. It's nerve-wracking to stand up on a stage like a tenor about to test his voice.

I cleared my throat. "Trinardier, Albert." He got up and walked toward me. Nice kid, Trinardier. We had spent a year together and hardly knew each other. I was aware that he'd pasted pictures of Johnny Mathis in his notebook and a big one of Salvadore Allende, snipped from a magazine. I knew that he was fond of poetry. He'd written a paper on Hemingway. Right now he was wearing the same pair of corduroys he had worn in October. I shook hands with him for the first time. And that's stupid, too. We'd been together for a whole year, and just when we'll stop seeing each other, we shake hands. I handed him his book.

"Goodbye, sir."

I was unexpectedly moved. I wanted to call him by his first name, just once.

"Goodbye, Trinardier, Albert."

Everyone laughed, a little embarrassed. That's just like me: I never have the nerve to follow through. I crack a little joke and let it go at that. I hope he understood. Farewell, Albert.

"Caranel, Emilie."

They call her Caramel, naturally, Miss Caramel. She doesn't mind. She's cute, with reddish hair. She won second prize—she's mad about Baudelaire and Lautréamont.

She gave me a rough handshake, like a day laborer. "Goodbye, Monsieur Bernier."

"Goodbye, Miss Caramel." Her eyes glistened, then seemed to vanish. I had never realized she had such long lashes.

Three more came to get their books and I returned to my seat. My job was finished, mission accomplished.

The chairs, table and plants had been removed and the play was about to begin. It was almost eleven. Four scenes from *Andromaque*, the girls draped in sheets, their faces heavily made up. Pyrrhus in a toga that didn't quite conceal his sneakers.

It was a great success. There were lots of fans in the audience.

Things ended quickly enough. I finally drank my two

Ricards with Briette on the terrace of the café. I must have shaken a hundred hands. "Have a nice holiday," "Have a good time," "See you in September." I went out into the sun, a bit befuddled by the drinks. Crowds of people thronged the boulevards; women's heels clicked under the chestnut trees. I came home feeling a little sad but also gay. I had two months ahead of me, as empty as blank pages. I would have to fill them up.

# Anne

*I* TRIED to take a cold shower but nothing doing—at the first drop I turned on the warm. I couldn't help it, I'm too thin-skinned.

My last clean towel. It was time for the year to be over. I'll do the washing in October.

There I stood, wet and naked in front of the bathroom mirror. Well, let's see. Not fleshy, that's something. The hips a little heavy, true, but nothing to be alarmed about. Legs okay, no varicose veins. I quit playing soccer at fourteen but I still seem to have plenty of muscle. I punt with my left foot, kick with my right, and admire myself in the mirror. Everything considered, I'm satisfied. My chest looks good but I hate to see the hair on it turning gray. I was twenty-five twenty years ago, I mustn't forget that.

Stomach flat, torso arched, biceps powerful—no chance of winning first prize for Mr. Universe but, all in all, not too bad.

Funny, I can never stand in front of a mirror without acting like an idiot. I wonder how old I'll be before I stop. I'm sure Duverrier, the principal, doesn't play at Tarzan in his bathroom.

Orange shorts. There I was plainly influenced by the ads. I've waited so often at the Richelieu-Drouot métro in front of a huge poster showing three beefy tanned young men in colored shorts drinking whiskey on a yacht that I finally succumbed and bought these orange ones. It was like embarking on a new life. Anyway, my holiday was beginning, a good time to start out with something new—the yacht could come later.

The shower cleared my head, and I decided I might as well finish the Dubonnet. There was just a little left. I keep the Dubonnet in the buffet for my personal use. To visitors I serve whiskey, to be more with it, but when I'm alone I drink Dubonnet. I think I can really qualify as the average Frenchman: 162 pounds, five feet eight, slightly bald, a little nearsighted, a schoolteacher who poses in front of his mirror—and who possesses the not very unusual name of Jacques Bernier.

One o'clock and I still had lots to do: ask the concierge to forward my mail, pay my rent, pay my telephone bill, but mainly pack my bags, or rather one suitcase. And then check the damn battery.

The suitcase, to begin with. I find it depressing to open my closet door. All my suits are gray, my shirts white, my sweaters dark, my shoes black. Actually the one colored thing I own is that pair of shorts, a bright note on my rear end. I might at least have treated myself to a snappy shirt. I'll arrive on the Riviera looking like an undertaker's assistant.

Occasionally I feel tempted to buy something really up-to-the-minute but such things are usually sold in some small select shop, a mere hole-in-the-wall, with Swedish salesgirls and strapping young customers who look like screenwriters. So naturally I hesitate. And then there are the students to consider. After I bought my boots, I taught all my classes glued to my desk chair instead of walking over to the blackboard as I usually do. Not that they were so showy, but they did have golden buckles and looked a little like cowboy boots. When I took the stairs four at a time I was convinced the entire school was staring at me.

The bell rang. It was Madame Morfoine, the concierge. She brought me one letter, a canceled check from the bank. She apparently wanted to chat. Usually she never came up unless she had at least five letters to deliver.

"Well, Monsieur Bernier, you're leaving?"

"Yes, indeed, Madame Morfoine, tomorrow morning."

She eyed my open suitcase on the floor. "You teachers are lucky. Two and a half months!"

"True, Madame Morfoine, one of the fringe benefits of the profession . . ."

"Where are you going, if I'm not being too curious?"

That's the way she talks. She's quite capable of asking, "And how many women in your life, if I'm not being too curious?"

"To the Midi, above Menton, a little village . . ."

An acid smile hovered over her blade-thin lips. "You'll have plenty of sun there."

"I hope so, Madame Morfoine."

She stood there for a moment thinking of something to say and I had a sinking feeling that she'd remain riveted to the spot forever.

"Now that I think of it, would you mind forwarding my mail?"

With Anne's address and a ten-franc note clenched in her fist, she left. The steps creaked under her weight and I poured myself a Dubonnet. I was glad I'd be seeing Anne again.

When she was little, it was always hard to leave her on Sunday evenings when I'd bring her back to her mother. I used to take her to see the Walt Disneys. For three years, from the time she was seven, she never missed a single Disney film. Although they were hard to take,

I often had to sit through them twice. Once we saw *Peter Pan* three times in succession, eating licorice all the while. I was sick that night. She was fine.

During the summer months I'd take her to the zoo in the Bois de Boulogne. The time I've spent standing in front of the bears! She never tired of them. At ten she began to ask to see love stories. Whenever *Gone with the Wind* was being shown, she'd wave the amusement section of the paper in front of me. Off we'd rush to the métro. I must have seen that movie at least once in every single *arrondissement* of Paris. I know it by heart. Even today I can recite the dialogue, my eyes closed. I'm an expert on the complicated loves of Rhett Butler and Scarlett O'Hara.

I would bring her back at eight-thirty. "Good-night, Anne, see you next week."

"See you Sunday, Papa."

For my birthday she would give me a drawing, and I still have all eleven of them. I've sorted them out: the first is of a house with green sun and a strange object with slender legs that she claimed was a lamb. The last is a charcoal drawing of a dancer, very carefully executed, full of shading, and signed with a flourish: *Anne*. It was clever but the colors have almost disappeared; she was sixteen at the time.

Then one day my ex-wife, Catherine, announced she was leaving for Canada "to start a new life," as she put it. I had shared her life for a year and a half, a brief enough period, but one that had seemed as endless to her as it did to me. She hesitated to take Anne with her, to another country, a new language, a different world. She had some friends over there in Toronto who would put her up, could she ask me to . . .

In short, Anne came to live with me. I moved, we repainted the apartment, she pasted pictures all over the walls, treated herself to a record player, the years passed.

Anne the schoolgirl, Anne the college student, Anne in love, Anne gone.

A postcard from India during the holidays, a phone call from time to time, the Algerian restaurant on the Rue de Bièvre where I would treat her, whenever she was free, to a couscous washed down with a small bottle of strong wine. We lead parallel lives at the moment. She has done very well. I watch for the credit titles on television and see her name quite often—stage designer: Anne Bernier. That pleases me. But our worlds rarely touch. She lives at a pace that takes my breath away, I couldn't possibly keep up.

Then, three weeks ago, as we ate our steaming couscous, she placed her elbows on the checkered tablecloth. "How would you like to spend your vacation with me?"

"If you promise you won't take me to *Gone with the Wind*."

She laughed. She's beautiful when she laughs, far more beautiful than her mother. And she knows how to dress, unlike me.

Then she told me about the house, a short distance from Sainte-Agnès, in the hills, with a marvelous view and no sound except crickets. I could rest, read, work if I wanted to. Of course Frédéric would be there but . . .

"Do you like Frédéric?"

"Yes, I do." It was true, I have nothing against Frédéric. The only thing I resent is that he sleeps with my daughter, but that's just the old-fashioned side of my nature.

"So will you come? Say yes. You'll have a terrific room on the second floor, the garden's full of flowers . . ."

It would have been hard to refuse.

"Besides, we've never spent a vacation together."

I raised a glass full of purple wine. "To our vacation!"

We parted in a gay mood, delighted with one another. Ye gods! It was almost four and I hadn't finished packing! Socks on top, four pairs should be enough. I'd be wearing sandals most of the time, so why take anything extra?

Would I need a sweater? It's pretty hot down there but on cool nights I might be glad to have it. The bag was closed. Well, that was done. I should have swept the place but I felt lazy. The morning's ordeal had worn me out.

Now what about the car? I knew I had plenty of gas but was worried about the battery. And with 87,000 kilometers on the odometer, I had the feeling that when I topped a rise in the road the car would drop from sheer exhaustion, would suffer some sort of heart attack.

The fact is, I'm terrified of my car. I keep thinking that this old three-h.p. Citroën is just waiting until I'm caught in heavy traffic to stop once and for all, everyone honking furiously, cops blowing their whistles, and me trying to disappear from view behind the wheel. It's still running, true, but what about tomorrow?

I could have taken the train, bought a sleeper. I would have arrived on the Riviera the next morning fresh and pink-cheeked among the palm trees. Instead of which I'll be stuck to my seat, dripping with sweat in the hot interior of my car, risking death every second, on the alert for suspicious noises in the engine: the squeaks, groans, hiccups that are bound to occur after the first twenty kilometers. It was a question of expense. I can well afford to travel by train but neglected to make a reservation: I had completely forgotten. Anyway, Meunier, Carnot or someone else assured me it was ridiculous to go by train if you owned a car. They knew of cars that had been driven as much as 150,000 kilometers. Besides, this year's holiday departure dates will be staggered so everyone won't be leaving at the same time. All this gave me a fleeting feeling of self-confidence. For a while I managed to convince myself that it's pleasant to drive: the exhilaration of speed, the sense of freedom, the feeling that you can stop anywhere, anytime . . . But now that I'm about to take off, my palms are sweating at the thought of having to drive over 1,000 kilometers in a junk heap with burnt-out cylinders.

I'll never make it. If I get as far as Fontainebleau it'll be a miracle. I downed another glass of Dubonnet. It's foolish to let oneself get worked up.

I decided to fix some spaghetti. There was a little bit of chopped beef left from lunch. I'll mix it all up and put myself in an Italian mood. Sainte-Agnès is only a few miles from the border.

I lit a cigarette and saw that I had only a few Gauloises left. What if I tried to quit smoking over the vacation? I'll be out in the open; I should take advantage of the fresh air to clean out my lungs. Anne had often warned that smoking was bad for me. She had been impressive when she talked about it, using terrifying words like heart attack, cancer, emphysema. I really must try. I would buy one more package tomorrow morning for the road but as soon as I got there I would stop.

Also, I planned to get some much needed exercise. For the past ten years I had intended doing something of the sort. I could see myself running over the thyme and the rosemary, climbing the hills in the soft early morning air: hiking, broad-jumping, jogging, one-two, one-two . . . I would come back tanned, rested, strong, with lungs clean and free of nicotine. I could hear fat old Rebolot on my return: "Well, my dear Bernier, you look twenty years younger!"

The water for the spaghetti was boiling. I dropped in the long strands and watched them twisting in the pot. Then I grated the Swiss cheese. I would go to bed early. I'd set the alarm for five, maybe even for four-thirty. A quick shave, the suitcase shoved in the trunk, and off I'd go, taking the Boulevard Raspail onto Denfert-Rochereau, then heading straight toward the Porte d'Orléans to reach the autoroute. It would take me all the way to Avignon. Nothing could be easier. Then across Provence to Anne's. She'd be waiting at the door of her house, I hoped, just like in a Walt Disney movie.

Plate, fork, knife, and I was ready to eat. It was only five o'clock, but I like to eat at any old hour when I don't have to go to the school cafeteria. Besides, I hadn't eaten since noon.

I planned to read a little, but I wouldn't call anyone to say goodbye; I would send postcards after I got there. As for the battery, I would check it tomorrow morning to make sure it had enough water: there was nothing else I could do.

Outside, the white sun beat against my window. The Parisians were going to fry this summer; the city would be like an oven, unbearable. They'd be furious. The very thought made me laugh—I must have a mean streak. Tomorrow at this hour I would be far away.

# *Pescarolo*

*I* DIOT! Moron! That's typical of people who drive those huge Peugeot 404s. They're all bastards, they all have the same sullen pig faces, the same contemptuous look in their eyes. And they all weigh at least three hundred pounds.

All that to-do just because I passed a gigantic trailer that was dragging along at fifteen kilometers an hour—there was nothing else on the road I could pass and I wasn't about to deprive myself of the pleasure. I had signaled, pulled out to the left—when that moron appeared on the horizon like a meteor, banging on his horn, blinking his lights—the works. You'd think he was dying to hit me, to drive me off the road! I swerved, calmly, and by the time I was back in the right lane he was probably in Marseille.

I've managed to get beyond Fountainbleau after all, but one thing bothers me: this old heap is running magnificently. My ears are on the alert for signs of trouble but there's not the slightest suspicious noise, no creaks, groans, no trace of anything burning. It's eating up the road like a champion, keeping to a steady ninety, heading straight for the Riviera as if fresh off the assembly line. That's what worries me more than anything else.

25

Everything's going too well. When disaster strikes, it will be a whopper. Like in the Westerns, everything's quiet, the guys are playing their harmonicas and suddenly, with a yell, on come the Indians!

In any case, leaving the city proved remarkably easy. Nothing on the streets except a few early morning bikes. It was cool, a gentle breeze stirred the sheets of a newspaper in the gutter, there was some heavy traffic around Alésia and the fork at Orly, but for the last half hour the road has been clear, empty, and damn monotonous. The autoroute is convenient but it's a terrible bore.

Lyon, 380 kilometers. It's going to be hot, all right: I can already feel the sun through the windshield, through my nylon shirt. And it's only a little after eight.

Now what about treating myself to a Gauloise for the road? Just one for the start of the holiday. Come on, it's a small pleasure, but a delicious one. The gray-blue smoke floats off in the yellow light. The road is straight, I have two fingers on the wheel, a cigarette on my lips, an eye on the rearview mirror, and I'm on top of the world.

And how about a little music? The radio sounds like an asthmatic with a cold but sometimes a tune comes through.

> *Aime-moi, aime-moi*
> *Quand je suis dans tes bras*
> *Je dis: Oh! la la la la la la*
> *Aime-moi, aime-moi . . .*

Unbearable. I've seen the singer on television, a big tired blonde, who swings her behind as if she had a nest of wasps lodged there. Some of my students have pasted her picture in their copybooks. That's the sort of thing that really makes you feel the generation gap.

*. . . three kilometers of blocked traffic at Nogent-le-*

*Rotrou, better detour to Emeraude route. A slowdown at Vienne, but everywhere else cars are moving at an even clip, good driving for the vacationers, the sun is in a holiday mood, life is beautiful, the sea is blue, in ten minutes we'll have another report—you are listening to Johnny here . . .*

The hearty voice of the announcer gives me an inferiority complex. He must be full of vigor, with a perpetual smile that reveals his flawless snow-white teeth. He probably drives around in a streamlined convertible with gorgeous girls in the back seat, all laughing gaily like the ones in the Coca-Cola ads.

I've had enough of the damn radio.

Careful now, I'm about to pass. A quick look at the rearview mirror—no huge purring Peugeot 404s in sight— here goes!

I catch a glimpse as I shoot by. At least thirty people in that Simca, puny kids all piled on top of each other! And the guy at the wheel, staring at the blue hills of the Vosges, looks tense, like a *poilu* left over from World War I. The rack on top of the car is a sight to behold— all sorts of suitcases, a small bike, a baby carriage with its wheels in the air, huge bags lashed down with a canvas cover. The floorboard practically touches the ground. They'll never make it. Three cheers for vacation time!

Next gas station, 25 kilometers. I'll stop and fill up. My second Gauloise.

The old heap keeps moving along like greased lightning. It's eating up the road and showing not the slightest sign of trouble. I'm so calm and relaxed I feel like singing.

Three-car caravan ahead. Pull over, boys, the road belongs to me, I'm passing. One . . . two . . . three, and that's it! Three at a time. I'm unbeatable. My real name is Fangio—no, he's too old. Who is the world's racing champion nowadays? A name I've often heard—Italian-sounding . . . Pescarola! Yes, that's it, Pescarola. I don't really know if he's the champion, but what difference does it make? I am Pescarola at the wheel of his Lola. Anyway, I'm in top form, no question about it.

Wait a minute, the gas station. Not too many people, at least not at the "Regular." It's not always easy to find one of those. Sometimes I think I'm the only person who doesn't use "Premium." I guess I'll stop here for a minute and limber up my legs. I part with thirty francs—gas is getting more expensive every day—and park my racer in the half empty lot, in front of a shop that looks like a branch of the Galeries Lafayette. These autoroutes are amazing; their service stations look more and more like sprawling shopping centers.

My legs felt a bit stiff as I got out. The weather was beautiful. It had been such a long time since I'd had the sun on my face I'd forgotten how good it feels. I stared at the store window in front of me and suddenly I spotted *it*.

I thought I was too old for love at first sight. But here it was, exactly what I wanted: a simple, two-button suit, blue denim, stitched pockets and wide-bottomed trousers —perfect! A quick glance at the price, an old penny-pinching habit—150 francs, a price I could afford.

I could hardly breathe. Usually it takes me three weeks to make up my mind between a black-and-white check at one department store and a brown synthetic at another. To buy something like this on the autoroute without first mulling it over—that had never happened to me before.

I looked into the shop. There was only one saleswoman, and thank heaven she didn't look like an emancipated Swede. I decided to go in. It would be nice to arrive on the Riviera wearing something new. Anne would be delighted, Frédéric amazed, and anyway, it's vacation time.

I entered. She approached me quietly, not at all forbidding. I can count on the fingers of one hand the number of saleswomen who don't intimidate me.

"I'd like to see the suit in the window, the blue one for a hundred fifty francs."

"Certainly, I'll be happy to show it to you." She thought it quite natural that I wanted it, and darted a covert look at the charcoal-gray suit I was wearing. "It's very light and comfortable. A hot summer is ahead and you've picked a popular model." She pulled out a tape measure and measured my waist.

"Will it wear well?" I asked, just to say something. Actually, I couldn't have cared less.

"Very well. The denim is of fine quality. Would you like to try it on?"

No time was lost. Alone in the dressing room with the object of my desire, I held it in my arms. Dressing rooms panic me, they're very dangerous places: the curtains have a way of sliding along the rod, leaving sizable gaps. I always have the feeling that a hundred old ladies are peering into the openings, spying on my thin legs, poking each other at the sight of my crumpled socks, jeering at the spectacle of my shirt tail flapping over my read end.

Very methodically, I proceeded to remove my shoes, then my trousers, which I tossed into a heap on the floor. I pulled on the new pair, all fresh and airy, zipped up the fly, and examined myself. Perfect! Now the jacket.

Was this really me? I felt unbelievably buoyant, elegant, nonchalant. The suit was a marvel—a perfect cross between the career diplomat and the Arizona cowboy.

"It fits you perfectly. It doesn't require the slightest alteration."

I grinned sheepishly. "I admit I'm tempted. But don't you think that it's a little—what?—too youthful?"

Her brown eyes widened in astonishment. "Not at all! It's becoming and you're just the type to wear it. It's both practical and dressy. Yesterday a man bought the same model and he was at least sixty. I wouldn't hesitate a minute if I were you."

Sixty! That did it. "I'll take it." I surprised myself, never believing I could act so decisively.

"Wouldn't you like to wear it?"

That woman was full of good ideas. "Yes, it's going to be hot, and as you say . . ." I returned to the dressing room, gathered up my old trousers and jacket and handed them to her. Together they must have weighed a hundred pounds. How could I have worn that repulsive, dreary outfit for such a long time? I transferred keys, wallet, and pen to the new trousers and wrote a check, imagining all the while that I now looked like Cary Grant in the nineteen forties.

While she wrapped the package we chatted. The shop was doing very well. People stopped here for gas. The women would go to the rest rooms first, but on coming out would peek into the shop. Once inside, they bought just about anything, from knickknacks to synthetic mink coats. Of course business was not nearly as brisk in the winter.

Two customers entered. "Goodbye, Madame."

"Goodbye, Monsieur, and thank you."

I went out into the sun, walking on air. My fourth Gauloise. I felt like doing a tap dance. This was definitely a gala day. The car was behaving, the battery was holding up, I had just bought a fantastic outfit, the weather was gorgeous, I was going to see Anne, I had dropped twenty years. Yippee!

I drove off. As soon as I turned on the ignition the car leaped forward like a thoroughbred. The traffic was heavy in Vienne; at Lyon, too, there was a jam. I got stuck in the wrong lane on the way to Grenoble, but now I had it made, the road ahead was clear!

Valence, 42 kilometers.

It was almost two o'clock. Curiously enough, I was starved, something that hadn't happened to me in a long time. Ordinarily, I eat without zest—whether in the school cafeteria, at home or in a restaurant. But now, all of a sudden, I craved something delicious. I didn't know exactly what—maybe a green salad with tomatoes, a small bottle of dry rosé and a grilled steak. Something light so I wouldn't fall asleep at the wheel, but substantial. I had thought of buying a sandwich at the parking lot but decided against it. After all, I'm on vacation and I'd like to celebrate properly.

I drove for another thirty kilometers until I saw a blue poster picturing a plate with knife and fork crossed. Just looking at it whetted my appetite.

And here I was, facing the window, resplendent in my new suit. The sun literally flooded the room, making the plexiglass tables sparkle. The decanter of rosé glistened, my plate was heaped high with salad of rice, olives, hard boiled eggs, and little cubes of something I didn't recognize. The whole thing was absolutely delectable. Waitresses in black miniskirts with red crepe-paper aprons rushed up and down the aisles. The place was jammed, the strains of soft music filled the air, and I had only 150 kilometers to Avignon. Then I'd be off the autoroute and the rest would be easy. The worst was over.

The salad was sheer delight! I gobbled it as if I was famished. A heavy-set man with a worried look on his face approached my table.

"May I sit down?"

I gulped another mouthful. "Certainly."

He was in a hurry. In a voice full of fury he ordered sausage and sauerkraut and immediately launched into a discussion of radiators.

"Are you having trouble with your radiator?"

Frankly, I don't even know whether my car has a radiator. During the course of numerous conversations about cars I long ago concluded that mine must have been shortchanged. I assume it has a motor, but I can't even swear to that. I rarely raise the hood.

"No, everything seems all right," I answered offhandedly.

He looked disappointed and started in on his sausage so disconsolately that I felt twinges of guilt.

"Now that you mention it, it's my battery that worries me," I volunteered.

He stopped eating, his fork in the air. "How old is your battery?"

Frantically, I searched my memory. "About five years."

He made a sound like air bursting from a balloon and snorted authoritatively: "Well, it's a goner. I buy one every three years."

I hadn't expected such a blow. So my battery is as good as dead! Fortunately my grilled steak arrived in time to lift my spirits. Trying to sound as if I knew something about cars, I said "It's still pretty good. One of these days I'll have to replace the points." I had heard Carnot say something of the sort often enough and was rather pleased to have hit upon it. But I must have slipped up: my luncheon partner eyed me suspiciously. "What kind of car do you have?"

"A three-horsepower Citroën."

He emitted a hollow grunt and returned to his sauerkraut. I finished eating quickly, paid the bill and left, but not before wishing him good luck on his trip.

That fellow was crazy to claim that my battery is done for! Some people take malicious pleasure in trying to cut the ground from under you.

I treated myself to an after-dinner smoke, inserted the key in the ignition and turned on the motor. It started like a charm. First, second, third, fourth, and I was already hitting seventy-five. He'd do better to see to his radiator instead of attacking my battery.

I turned on the radio. A pop group was singing but I left the damn thing on. When you wear an outfit like mine, you have to be a swinger. I started to whistle.

# Jesus Christ

*B*UT after all, Anne wasn't waiting for me at the door.

I arrived under a yellow setting sun that lit up only the round-tiled roofs, the church tower, the steep hills in the distance. I had to ask the way three times. At the last stop, a short old man dressed in black switched his basket from one hand to the other and leaned on my door, filling the car with an aroma of figs and grapes.

"I see where you want to go. When you leave the village there'll be a narrow road on your left, just before the wash house. Keep going a short way and you'll see a house part way up the hill. Take care, the goats are usually brought in at this time of day, you might run into a troop of them. They're not very smart animals."

I thanked him and drove off. I was completely exhausted after twelve hours at the wheel. That's a lot, especially for me. I realized now that for the last hundred kilometers I had been driving automatically, from sheer habit. I must have clipped a few corners. On leaving Villefranche I had gone into a controlled skid, quite by accident, and felt stupidly pleased with myself. Before that I'd had an adventure at Sainte-Maxime. Traveling at a good rate after a traffic jam at Sénas, near the top of a

rise in the road I saw the figure of a young girl outlined
against the pure gold of the sky. She was hitchhiking:
sweater, slacks, duffel bag at her feet. There was something melancholy and charming about her slender silhouette.

I didn't think for a minute that she might rub her
leg against mine, wriggle her torso and end up with me
in the shelter of some Provençal grove. But of course
I've heard such tales and I suppose some of them must be
true.

I stopped. The hitchhiker came over and asked me in
a low-pitched voice: "Could you take me as far as Nice?"

Only then did I notice that my hitchhiker sprouted a
few days' growth of beard and had a flat chest. The long
hair style is most confusing.

I swallowed my disappointment and the fellow settled
down next to me. A very nice guy, as it turned out. We
smoked a few Gauloises and talked about life. He had
traveled a lot. He knew all there was to know about Peru,
whereas I at his age had never ventured beyond the
Seine-et-Marne. He was hoping to specialize in com-
parative linguistics. In the end I was sorry to see him
get out to join a group of his friends. His hair came down
to the middle of his back and his general appearance
would have made Madame Morfoine pop out of her room,
demanding shrilly: "No hippies on my stairs!"

The road the old man had indicated was a winding,
climbing affair covered with sharp stones. My tires being
thin, I began to get worried when suddenly I spotted the
farmhouse.

I pulled over and walked the rest of the way. What
struck me as eerie was the silence—the first I had en-
countered in a year. Like butter, the sun spread over the
last mountain crests, the heavy scent of thickly growing
plants pervaded the region, and the air was soft and
translucent like some old, beloved melody. I walked past

a pepper plant, followed a twist in the road and saw the door. It was then that I felt a twinge of disappointment. Anne wasn't there.

Instead, a young man sat on the steps. Stripped to the waist and barefooted, he was fiddling with a piece of wire. For a moment I thought I had come to the wrong place.

He raised his head to look at me, seeming only mildly surprised.

"Does Anne Bernier live here?" I asked.

He took his time, twisting the wire, before replying, "Yes."

I can't stand people like that. You ask a question and the guy continues to finish what he's doing before bothering to answer.

"I'm her father." As soon as I'd spoken I realized how ridiculously solemn I sounded. The big lout didn't seem a bit impressed, and rightly so. Moving his long lanky legs to one side to let me pass, he shook my hand. "Greetings. I'm Max."

His handclasp was firm and I was smiling like an idiot when Anne appeared, looking radiant. She was wearing a sweat shirt and khaki skirt. She kissed me on both cheeks and hurried me inside. "I'm so happy you're here! Come on in, you must be absolutely exhausted."

I'm always happy when I'm holding her close. "You guessed it. I really am dead tired."

It was so dark I could barely distinguish a few benches, some pots of paint, and a crowd of young men and women lying on mats on the floor. I thought there were at least a hundred of them.

"I'll go make you some coffee, sit down. Some friends are here with me."

From the mats, a few arms waved limply—a gesture of welcome, I supposed. I responded in kind and sank onto a bench. It was then that a forgotten phrase of Anne's came back to me.

I remembered that at the end of the meal in the restaurant on the Rue de Bièvre she had said something, a few quick words to which I had attached no importance at the time, something like, "Some friends of mine will probably be there," but it was submerged by the usual avalanche of words. Anne is so incredibly voluble, it's hard to get a single word in. At any rate, she had talked so much that I had completely forgotten this detail. Now, after driving twelve hundred kilometers, I found myself face to face with that detail: I had stumbled upon a commune.

I looked them over as I drank my coffee and answered Anne's questions. A gigantic girl in a lonk skirt was lying flat on her stomach, attempting to read in the last faint rays of light, a boy's woolly head cushioned on her buttocks.

"Did you have any engine trouble?"

"No, the car drove beautifully."

She drew back her head as if to contemplate a painting and clasped her hands. "Why, you've bought a new suit!"

I nearly choked over my coffee. I stammered: "Yes, it was so hot, I thought I . . ."

She kissed me again. "You look wonderful!" Then she turned and called out, "Kim, will it be ready soon?"

Kim poked her head through the window. I hadn't seen her before. A tiny, curly-haired redhead, she was brandishing a wooden soup ladle. "It's cooking," she answered. "We'll eat in five minutes."

"Come and meet my father. This is Kim Spander, you must have seen her on television."

I shook hands with Kim, who was still clutching her ladle. At this point, Frédéric came in. Sporting an Indian shirt, he carried a cardboard folder full of drawings. Max followed, still intent on his brass wires.

"Hello, Monsieur Bernier. Did you have a good trip?"

I had no time to answer. Anne grabbed me and we

dashed off together toward the staircase. "Come and take a look at your pad. If you want to wash up, everything's ready for you."

The room was magnificent, small but really magnificent: red tiled floor, whitewashed walls, a big old brass bedstead, a peasant commode, a table in front of the window, and two straw-bottomed chairs.

She looked at me. "Well?"

"Wonderful!" I shouted.

She laughed. "Did you bring any papers to correct?"

It was my turn to laugh. "No, I've finished all my chores and don't have a thing to do. Are there any books around?"

"The room next door is full of them. You can't get any in the village, but Menton is only twenty-five kilometers away. You'll find whatever you want there. Let me show you the bathroom."

"Wait a minute, I left my bag in the trunk. I'll go get it."

She crossed the room and leaned out of the window. "Frédéric, will you bring Papa's valise?"

"I can get it, I'm not seventy yet," I protested.

She gestured like a protective mother. "You're tired. Why don't you take a bath? You'll find everything there you need. We'll eat soon. Kim has cooked beef *en daube*. I told her that's what you like. If you need anything, shout."

She was already at the door when I timidly remarked: "There are so many of you!"

"Ten with you."

Of course that wasn't a hundred, but to me it seemed like a lot.

"See you."

All in, I stared at the tub. After closing the door, I looked at myself in the round mirror above the washbasin. A vague commotion reached my ears, the sound of plates, laughter, and one girl's voice in particular braying loudly.

Good lord! I felt sorry for myself—I, who loathe large groups! Here I am, the asocial type, catapulted into a vacationers' colony. I've been ambushed, trapped! Well, we'll see how it goes, but if it weren't for Anne I'd already be far away. Of course, if it weren't for Anne I would never have come in the first place. I might have known that she can't live without five hundred people around her.

The shower refreshed me. Now I'll stretch out in the tub and let the water run over my body. It feels so good, I could drop off. Sleep comes gently, the colored bath tiles gradually blur, the lingering whitish light grows darker, then disappears . . .

> *AIME-MOI, AIME-MOI*
> *QUAND JE SUIS DANS TES BRAS*
> *JE DIS: OH! LA LA LA LA LA LA*
> *AIME-MOI, AIME-MOI*

I splashed the entire wall and almost bashed my head against the soap dish. That, without doubt, was the loudest record player I'd ever heard. There were shouts of protest, then the volume was lowered. I soaped myself languidly, rinsed myself off and contemplated my nude body, my mind a total blank.

Tap, tap, tap on the bedroom door. I leaped up, bumped my head again, and hurriedly wrapped a flowered towel around my waist.

"Uh . . . come in."

It was the gigantic girl in the long dress. She was carrying my bag. "Oh, sorry, I brought you your suitcase."

"That's fine, thank you." I clutched the towel. Unlike me, she seemed entirely at ease.

"My name is Françoise."

It was a good thing she didn't hold out her hand. I must have looked like an idiot. Who would have thought last night that I would find myself practically naked in the company of a giantess? Actually, and this seemed odd, she looked shorter standing than lying down.

"Well . . . I'm Bernier, Jacques Bernier."

She grinned, exposing pearly teeth, then gestured, a kind of military salute. Without thinking, I imitated her but managed to grab my towel in time and sat down, exhausted. Too much novelty for a man like me. I put on my shirt and trousers and, throwing caution to the winds, discarded my socks for the evening meal.

I descended the vaulted stairway, which had a roughhewn stone ceiling. My throat felt tight. No wonder. I'd fallen among hippies.

The introductions took place while the beef *en daube* was being served to the sound of scraping benches. I already knew Max, the man with the brass wires. I learned afterward that the little objects he was forever constructing were models for abstract sculptures that sell very well in the United States. This staggered me. It would never have occurred to me to earn a living by twisting brass wires around bits of wood. Max is a taciturn boy, very sure of himself.

From time to time, always when you least expected it, Kim, the dancer, would execute a split or leap into the air, kicking her legs. Françoise, the giantess, worked in a shop. There were two bearded Christs, Antoine and Virgil. One of them had a girl, a bohemian type enveloped from head to toe in a black wool shawn. She kept staring at me as if at any moment I might crumble into dust.

From the other end of the table, Anne called to me "How do you like our pad?"

I gulped down a mouthful of food and tried desperately

to think of an original answer. You really have to impress
these young people.

"I think it's wonderful. You couldn't get me to stay
anywhere else."

One of the Christs snickered. "Me too. I'm going to
stay here until December."

Laughter. They all talked at once. "Put on a record,"
Frédéric suggested.

Françoise swayed off toward one end of the room.
Kim shouted something I couldn't make out. Anne was
happily chatting with Frédéric. I gathered they were
talking about a movie: a chap called Pierre was supposed
so come and see if this place was right for shooting a
scene. That's all we needed, some film producers. Behind
me an orchestra exploded, the drummer seemed to be
banging on my temples.

The bohemian's voice rose above the hubbub. "You're
a prof?"

Careful! Dangerous territory. "Yes."

"How can anyone be a prof in times like these?"

The conversation around us continued. Anne, sitting
opposite the steaming soup pot, laughed merrily.

I shouted: "Well, sometimes it is difficult, but I manage
to survive each year until the end of June."

She seemed surprised and Max's head bobbed up. "I
thought the kids shoot at you as you enter the classroom."

"It hasn't happened yet. Maybe next year."

Frédéric picked his teeth with his fingernail. "Do your
students read Mao? He says that if a teacher's a bore,
the pupils have every right to fall asleep in his class."

Françoise protested: "But it's not a question of right,
it's a necessity. I often slept in class at the university."

That was all they needed. They were launched, and of
course I was forgotten in the din. I wouldn't last three
days in this atmosphere. The bohemian passed me the
Camembert and emptied her glass like a coal miner.

"You're not saying a word, Franz."

I too had forgotten him. He was an Austrian—round glasses, and three necklaces hung around his neck—who expressed himself in whispered monosyllables and followed a strictly vegetarian diet. He had been munching on celery for the last half hour, casting his eyes over everything with infinite sorrow.

Frédéric leaned back, the soles of his sneakers on the edge of the table. "Your turn to wash the dishes, Antoine."

Antoine protested, lit a cigar as bent and twisted as a twig, and I offered my services. I wanted to demonstrate my good will and communal spirit.

General demurral. I circulated my package of Gauloises.

Françoise left the bench to coil up in an armchair near the fireplace. "Have you seen Kenneth Anger's latest film? He's weird, that hombre!"

"No."

Virgil fingered his beard and stared at me sternly.

"You've got to see it, it's absolutely weird."

I didn't dare to divulge that I had treated myself to an entire week of the Fred Astaire festival. They wouldn't think him weird at all.

The place began to look like a North African bazaar. The bohemian and one of the Christs played a complicated game of cards. The others sprawled on the floor and talked in tired voices. Frédéric had installed Anne on his knees. The other Christ, his eyes closed, took up a yoga position. Kim cleared the table, still executing sudden leaps and entrechats. With simple grace, Franz caressed her legs as she passed but she paid no attention. Women have definitely changed.

A new record on the player: the Mammoths, a weird group.

I was of course bored, but I also feared—it's hard to put it in words—that one of them might become aggressive and bombard me with questions. I don't have their quick wit, and I don't quite understand their language, their jokes. They're probably very nice kids. Why don't they show it?

I glanced at my new slacks. They had given me the illusion of youth for a few hours, but it didn't last. Tonight I felt old. My back ached. At dinner I tried to sit up straight so I wouldn't look my age, but now, after that long exhausting trip, I was so done in I couldn't take it any longer.

"Excuse me," I said and got up. "I'm pretty tired. Good night, everyone!"

Anne came over and kissed me. "Do you want me to come and tuck you in?"

I shook my head. "Stay with your pals. I'll be in better shape tomorrow."

Still, a hint of anxiety lurked in her eyes, a flicker of worry. "What do you think of them?"

I forced my voice. "Likable, very likable." That reassured her. And it's true; they are likable. It's only that they and I live in different worlds, and even though I know they're quite harmless, their very presence seems an inexplicable threat.

Now I was alone in my room. Once again the old man was alone while below the children were playing. What are they saying about me right now? "He's not bad, your father." "He looked a little bewildered." "He doesn't seem very talkative." Or else, and this would be worse, they don't even mention me, as if I didn't exist. I could hear them laughing. They seemed to be having a better time since I left. I went right to sleep. The next day I was informed that they had gone to bed around four. Apparently it had been a really weird evening.

My anxiety was most acute when we assembled for meals. The rest of the time I could manage. I would go for a stroll in the hills, a whodunit in my pocket. I found a tree near the top of the slope and settled myself comfortably in its shade. The country around me resembled Colorado; the white rocks seemed to be leaning toward me. I thought I could see Italy some distance away, through a cleft in the ravine. I read four pages, dozed off and slept like a baby. The sun shifted while I slumbered and I acquired a mighty sunburn. Kim congratulated me on how well I looked.

"When you arrived," she told me, "you were the color of the evening paper."

We had already begun to use the intimate term *tu*. I'm not accustomed to this sort of thing but I liked it and was surprised at how easily I could adjust.

I spent a good part of the afternoon with Catherine, the bohemian. She came out and joined me under the fig trees, still wrapped in her black wool shawl, although it was eighty in the shade.

She was far from stupid. We talked about everything and nothing. She had read a lot, worked in various shops and also sold advertising. She had created, on the fringes of reality, a delicate feverish world of her own which struck me as grotesque, and also attractive.

I felt that if I had asked her to go to bed with me she would have accepted with disarming simplicity, as a favor you do for a member of your own crowd. In a friendly fashion we would have copulated under the hot Mediterranean sun. Of course I wouldn't have dreamt of suggesting it; this particular old man is too full of hang-ups.

The evening proved interminable. Virgil-Christ performed his act and everyone laughed, but for the life of me I couldn't understand what was so funny. The fixed smile on my face was making my muscles ache. I watched Anne play poker, pretending I understood the game, and once again I was the first to retire.

I had just fallen asleep when noises awakened me. The

giantess and her boy friend occupied the room next to mine; our beds were on either side of a common wall. It isn't easy for a pathetic bachelor to listen to that. An intense feeling of envy, of jealousy, took hold of me. These youngsters seemed to have an absolutely inexhaustible supply of energy, quite different in this respect from my generation. Apparently the giantess had a zest that matched her extraordinary height. I thought they would never finish. It was difficult to fall asleep. If all my nights were going to be like this, I would return even more exhausted than I had been on arrival.

Just as I was about to doze off, I had an idea: tomorrow, on some excuse or other, I would go into Menton. I needed to be alone for a while. The very thought elated me. Okay, that was settled: tomorrow I would be on my way to town.

# *Esposito*

*I* opened the shutters to a steel-gray sky. Clusters of soft leaden clouds seemed to rise from the mountains and form an impenetrable purplish cover. I breathed in the humid air and felt as if I were at the bottom of a cauldron. The leaves of the ivy on the walls rustled softly, as if in preparation for the strong winds that accompany these violent and sudden summer storms.

I could see Max sitting on the stone stoop just below me. He was paring bits of wood with a pen knife, devising a fragile construction that would challenge the laws of equilibrium. He didn't raise his head and I continued to inhale the moist air and to contemplate the gray metallic mountains. Even the sea was probably gray. Sometimes the Mediterranean plays at imitating the Channel.

The weather suited my plans, providing an additional reason for going off to buy some books. What was there to do in such weather except read?

As I dressed I heard Anne's car. Frédéric was driving. The motor stalled, there were shouts from some of the others, and finally they left.

I went downstairs. Anne appeared shortly afterward, yawning a dozen times and turned on the radio. I buttered my roll and told her I was going to Menton. I was afraid one of the crowd would want to come along but there were no candidates. Kim and Anne were discussing clothes when I went off.

Drops splattered on the windshield, sharp slaps of rain were swept off by the windshield wipers, cutting the dust. I heard a rumble of thunder over the sea; the rain stopped. I opened the window, allowing the damp air to enter. It smacked of solitude. An eternity since I had last been alone.

The countryside had changed quite a bit. Long ago, when I was a child, I had often come here. My mother used to take me to a square near the Casino. I remembered it quite well. There were trees with thick, rubbery leaves. Near the bench where my mother sat knitting, I would play by the hour. All around stood giant palaces surrounded by columns, very high, way over my head, cupolas, rotundas of every shape—it was Baghdad, Alexandria, Moscow, all rolled into one. I wondered who could be living in such fabulous, awesome places—probably princes, dressed in turbans and heavy brocades. Silent servants glided along the corridors, raising the heavy drapes to bring golden trays, and bowing very low before vague and mysterious figures whose delicate fingers were covered with heavy rings. Beyond, in the quivering sunlight, was Monte Carlo, where English ladies strolled, their blue-white curls masked by hair nets and purple-hooded capes. They smoked cigarettes that had a special exotic aroma.

At a turn of the road the shoreline appeared and my memories were shattered. Tall buildings concealed the seashore. Coming unexpectedly upon them, I was quite bewildered. The walls of these high-rises had invaded miles and miles of the old landmarks. Entire cities were spread out before me, vertical, all the way to the old town, which I couldn't yet see.

Riviera Beach, Sun Marina, glass and plastic restaurants gobbled up the sidewalks. There were rows and rows of parking lots, snack bars, record shops, night clubs. Whatever had become of the square of long ago?

Worst of all were the billboards that shamelessly announced: on display, seventy-five apartments, five-room studios, moderate prices, balconies with a view of the sea, garbage disposals— everything you needed to be happy! I parked the car and walked toward the old town.

Very few bathers were on the beach because of the bad weather. The Riviera should be seen under a hot sun and blue skies, but this morning Menton, its white walls yellowed to an ivory, looked like Ostende. The arcade was deserted and the tables of the cafés, still wet from the rain, were covered with tarpaulins.

I felt good. Smoking a Gauloise, my hands in my pockets, I sauntered along. Like an old salt, I would climb the stairs of the jetty and walk all the way to the sea wall. This particular area didn't appear to have changed much, but everything seemed a little diminished, or perhaps it was I who had grown—and also aged.

The beach which once seemed an endless desert was now a strip of rather dirty sand. The sea was smooth, the waves a mere ripple.

Over there a bridge had been built, a viaduct into the mountain. And the port must be new. Here was the beacon. The sea looked sickly, like cardboard, the color of a patient with fever. Not a single boat in sight, only one of those water bicycles, with a couple drifting in it disconsolately, their feet immobilized on the pedals. I took a deep breath, letting the air penetrate my lungs.

On the craggy rocks along the jetty a few fishermen were eying their lines. It takes more than a gray sky and a few rain drops to scare these types away. They wore the kind of tan plastic raincoats you see on construction workers. I like watching people fish though it's

not a very lively spectator sport. I usually stop to ex-
change a few words—all very trite, of course, but I
somehow enjoy it.

This time my fisherman was a small large-bellied chap
in khaki shorts, with legs like a soccer player's and a
Stalin-type mustache.

He gestured disgustedly toward his motionless bobber.
"It's been like this all morning."

I mumbled a word of sympathy. "Haven't you caught
anything?"

He grimaced and pointed to a plastic pail against his
right knee. In the clear water a tiny fish was swimming
around frantically. It looked like a sardine but I couldn't
swear to it. My idea of a sardine is something minus a
head in a can I usually cut my fingers on and then spill all
over my trousers.

"And yet they should be biting in this kind of
weather . . ."

He accepted the Gauloise I offered. I sat down beside
him on a flat rock that hurt my bottom. He at once began
to complain.

"This isn't really the sea here, it's a basin of hot water.
My idea of a place to fish is the Lot-et-Garonne. I have
a friend who catches terrific fish there—an average of
twenty-five pike a week. But my wife wanted to come
here, so that's what you get . . ." He stared with disgust
at the pathetic sardine and shook his head. "Besides,
it's not convenient, the camping grounds here are far
away. I need my car to transport all the gear and if I
don't leave early I get caught in a traffic jam and can't
find a place to park." He sucked on his mustache. "This
morning I thought I'd catch something because of the
storm, but just take a look up there."

I raised my eyes. The clouds over Italy seemed to be
breaking up and timid bits of blue appeared between the
gaps. Above the mountains there was a faint light, as if

the voltage were turned low, but you could already feel that the sun would break through and chase away the last shadows.

The fisherman was from Argenteuil. He worked in a bank at the Place des Ternes and commuted by train every day, it was more practical than driving his car, and a lot cheaper. Good God, how those Peugeot 404s guzzled gas!

At this point, I listened more attentively. He certainly looked like one of those drivers who could crush you to pieces. Maybe he was the ferocious one who had passed me on the autoroute. He talked and talked, but I no longer listened. Before me the sea took on color and the gray disappeared, giving way to a transparency that was not quite green and not quite blue.

How great I felt! Forgotten my commune of hippies and the night of audible orgy. But I had to think about buying some books. It was getting on toward noon and the shops would soon be closed.

"Well, I wish you better luck."

My companion scratched his stomach and sighed. "Thanks, but the way things are going, and with all the oil they keep dumping . . ."

I fled to escape from the lecture about pollution I knew was in the offing and headed back.

People had come out by this time, children running on the beach, young couples holding hands and strolling, some laughing and exchanging quick little kisses; they had probably met only a few days ago and already they were kissing! How quickly things happened nowadays, and how slow in comparison had been the vacation loves of my youth! We were all so heavily weighted down by repressed desires, but they are so light and casual—a touch and off they fly. I used to assume such complicated roles with girls. I respected them but I was also a hypocrite. At seventeen I played at being a man of the world;

I don't think I've quite become one even now. Boys today strike me as so much more mature, so at ease with themselves. When they see a woman they like, they just grab her, throwing tactics and strategy to the winds . . .

Maybe it's because they are better looking than I was; they seem taller, thinner, gayer. Maybe it's the food they eat, the sun lotions they use, all the sports they have. At any rate, whenever I see them I realize I'm becoming an envious old man. Suddenly I feel a thousand years old.

Supposing I put my mind to other things. Here's the bookstore—now I'm in my element. The best sellers and the literary prize winners are near the cash register. One glance at the new books and I head for the paperbacks. But they take up an entire wall; you have to crouch in the far right corner to examine the very latest ones.

I finally chose eight: two Balzacs, one Gide, one Cocteau to improve my mind a little, and four detective stories, two by Chandler, one by Westlake, and one by somebody I'd never heard of. I leafed through this last and it looked interesting. Besides it had a picture of a terrific girl on the cover. You have to keep up with the times. The cashier put everything in a large shopping bag, which made me look as if I were coming home from market. And I was, in a way. I had bought my ration of reading, it should last me a week. When I've used it all up, I'll come back for more. And now, what about treating myself to a lunch at a little restaurant?

The sun was still weak, my shadow on the sidewalk only a dim outline. As I neared the old town I entered a small bistro called Esposito; it was not yet crowded. I settled down at a tiny table between a Dutch family and some Spanish house painters, chose the prix-fixe lunch at sixteen francs, and ordered a small bottle of rosé.

The sea air had made me ravenous. I devoured the spaghetti bolognese, drank some coffee, smoked a Gauloise, and satisfied a sudden desire for a cognac. Then I gaily sauntered out, carrying my large bag. With the entire afternoon to kill, I was assailed by a familiar anxiety: what on earth could I do?

I walked to the Casino and there I got an inspiration. An extraordinary billboard outside featured a green-eyed mastodon, its enormous teeth stained with blood. With its huge dirty claws it was crushing a dozen buildings at one fell swoop. At the bottom of the billboard you could see some little guys running around in a panic. The monster was hugging a pleasant-looking young lady who did not seem quite at ease. I could sympathize with her. Off to one side was a square red notice that read: TWO O'CLOCK PERFORMANCE.

Not a second to lose. I rushed to the ticket window and went in as if I were heading a regiment.

# Tordo

*WITHIN the cellars, beneath the ancient vaults, the finishing touches are given to these cheeses that tomorrow will be shipped around the world.*

It was hard to see in the dark hall. The usherette poked the flashlight at my eyes like a storm trooper. I thought she would order me to confess my crimes.

There was hardly anyone in the theater—a few lovers here and there in the back rows, a few middle-aged habitués, and myself.

The scenes succeeded each other with agonizing slowness. Documentaries always bore me but this one seemed particularly exasperating. At the moment a dozen fellows in hospital gowns were taking forever to load their precious cheeses onto trucks, proceeding as cautiously as if they were placing premature infants into incubators.

The hall was immense, a regular mausoleum, an old-fashioned movie theater with cherubs that faded and reappeared with the ebb and flow of the light shed by the screen. I sank into my seat and sighed contentedly.

*They will remain in cold-storage warehouses for a time before being shipped to retail stores, where you will find them, to the delight of your palate. Their unique aroma will . . .*

That's the trouble with provincial movie houses. They show documentaries and cartoons, the lights go on, the usherettes sell frozen ice cream bars, the curtain comes down, goes up, and you have to sit and twiddle your thumbs, waiting. The hall will grow dark again, you think the show is about to begin and, bang! "Next week on this screen . . ." The curtain is again lowered, you're ready to scream with rage, you go to the toilet just to kill time and when you return the feature has already begun. You almost break your neck in the dark trying to find your seat.

"Oh, come *on!*"

I started. Who had said that? I sat up straight and spotted her.

She was sitting in the row just in front of me, three seats to my left. She was slouched down, her knees up, and the changing lights of the screen focused on the taut denim of her jeans. I knew only three things about her so far: she was bored with the story about cheese, she was blond, and she liked to lounge in a theater seat.

I sank back into mine gently.

*And thus, day after day, deep within this barren soil, the wondrous adventure of soft cheeses takes place . . .*

Triumphant music burst forth for the final scene: a flaming sun setting behind the Auvergne mountains.

## THE END

I applauded, I couldn't help it. Sometimes, as a matter of fact, I even surprise myself. I'm shy, I hate to be conspicuous, but suddenly, for no apparent reason, I do something idiotic.

Of course no one joined in, but the girl in front of me

began to laugh. She turned toward me as the lights went on.

I saw her face for the first time. She wasn't a young girl but a woman about thirty-five, very pretty I thought, although I wasn't too sure. Soft lips, a curl on her cheeks like a parenthesis. But it was her lips that struck me.

"You must be crazy about cheese!"

"I always carry a variety of brands on me, a different one in each pocket." Her teeth glistened as she laughed again. She turned back to face the screen and all I could see was the top of her head.

She wasn't here to pick someone up, I was quite sure of that. She simply wasn't the type. She crossed her legs and rested one ankle on her knee. An old espadrille dangled from her toes. I noticed that a cord at the heel was loose and about to fall off. She wore a blue military-looking shirt with patch pockets, not the kind of costume you'd expect if she were looking for a pick-up. In any case, for the moment, she seemed to have forgotten me.

Like a coal miner, the usherette trundled down the aisle pushing her wagon of frozen ice cream bars. She stopped close to the screen, cast a weary glance around the half-deserted house, and dejectedly pushed her cart up another aisle.

There was complete silence, as if we were all dead. Some old granny unwrapped a hard candy and the rustle of paper reverberated like thunder. The noise stopped abruptly. The poor woman must be sucking it quietly, terrified at having caused such a commotion.

A few coughs to the left of me and the lights were dimmed. Soft music.

This place is driving me up the wall! A few days ago I'd probably have just said, "I'm bored stiff" but the vocabulary of Anne and her friends was rubbing off on me.

Another ad: "The records you now hear are on sale

at the Discodisc Shop, 36 Avenue Gambetta."

I could still hear my near neighbor's laugh. It had been neither restrained nor forced, just a hearty, spontaneous laugh. She must be very poised and self-assured.

Also, she didn't hesitate to speak to me first, whereas I wouldn't have dared. Chalk up a point for her. Her espadrille was still dangling. By leaning to one side I could see that she was resting her head on her hand and yawning hard enough to dislocate a jaw.

I leaned back. How would it look if she caught me peeking at her? Come on, Bernier old boy, don't start to daydream. That woman is still young, beautiful, she can have any man she wants. What would she want with an over-forty prof?

The lights were extinguished. A thunder of cymbals and on the wide screen, in dripping scarlet letters, the title was projected: MONSTER FROM THE BEYOND. The show had begun.


Teresa Simpson, dressed in a diaphanous cream-colored dressing gown, was about to slip between raspberry-striped turquoise sheets when the telephone rang.

"Is that you, darling?"

"Yes. I'll be late getting home, my love, don't wait up for me. I'm needed at the laboratory."

"Don't worry, darling, everything is fine. I'm feeling very relaxed." (Actually, you could see her fingers shaking as if she had palsy. In an earlier scene she had dropped a huge stack of dishes. Subtle, this movie).

"Go straight to bed, darling. Tordo has escaped to the desert. You can sleep in peace." (Tordo is the name of the monster, don't ask me why.)

"I'm going right to sleep. See you soon, darling. Don't work too hard."

"I won't. Good night, Teresa."

She replaced the receiver, sighed, and went to bed.

I must explain that Teresa was the wife of a sort of scholarly playboy who was trying to perfect a weapon that would annihilate Tordo. As for the monster itself, it had no particular character, but a few minutes earlier it had pulverized the Empire State Building with one sweep of its arm. It also had a very unprepossessing countenance.

Teresa shut her eyes.

Something was about to happen. There it was! An immense shadow filled the entire screen and through the window you could see a gigantic eye pressed against the pane. Things were about to pop, the music throbbed, and suddenly, boom! Tordo went into action, smashing the window and seizing the young woman between his claws. Teresa screamed. My neighbor sat up straight in her chair and in spite of the racket I could hear her gasp.

While Tordo stepped over the block of houses, I leaned over and said dramatically: "Have no fear. I am here."

She turned toward me, a purple cast over her face from the light of the screen. "Do you think he's going to kill her?"

"I'd be surprised. We've only seen the first half."

Scene was following scene but we were no longer watching. I had a sudden desire to talk to her, to be with her, somewhere else, to quit this idiotic movie that no longer amused either of us. But to do so required more nerve than I had, more than I had ever had in all my life.

On the screen, things had quieted down a bit. Teresa's playboy husband was searching the devastated apartment to see if by chance he could find his beloved. He had looked everywhere except inside the bedtable drawers. His head in his hands, he finally broke down, murmuring, "Teresa . . . Teresa."

My heart was beating so hard I thought it would be heard above the sonorous music. I would have to act quickly; all my life I had missed so many opportunities, this time I was determined to see things through. If Frédéric or Max or the two Christs were in my shoes at this moment, they would have changed seats, taken her in their arms, whereas I . . . I leaned forward.

"Forgive me, but this movie is beginning to drive me up the wall—and you too, I think. Shall we go? Let me take you somewhere for a drink. I assure you I'm not trying to pick you up."

Never in my life had I been so proud of myself! For a moment I couldn't believe that it was I who had spoken. She said nothing at first. Then suddenly she stood up. "Okay."

We walked slowly out of the movie house. I felt punch drunk, like a boxer in the ring sensing the fight speed up. It was dark and she stumbled on the stairs. I took her arm and we descended together.

Outside everything was all yellow and blue. The sun was shining and summer was at its height.

She leaned against a wall and stood there a moment, her face upturned. Then she asked: "What time is it."

"Four-thirty."

She was tall, carried no bag, and suddenly it seemed that the sun only shone for her. She had that quality of absorbing all its radiance.

"I must come back here at five," she said. "My sister will be waiting to take me home because . . ."

She buried her hands in the pockets of her jeans, smiling more glowingly than ever, and added gaily, "I am blind."

"A glass of beer."

"Make it two."

Her eyes are light, reflecting the sea and also a corner of a parasol. But they can't see the parasol or the sea . . .

I felt amazingly calm. While we talked she laughed

several times. It's strange to be able to look at someone without being afraid they will think you are staring. I could examine her mouth, her forehead at my leisure while she drank her beer. A little foam had gathered on a corner of her lip. She put the glass down on the table, using her little finger as a guide, touching the surface without groping.

"Who are you?"

"Well, I . . . well, it's very simple, I'm a professor of French and right now I'm on vacation."

I sensed that she was still waiting. She could perhaps tell by the sound of my voice that I wanted to say more. Maybe you always want to say more to blind people to compensate a little for their affliction.

"I live in Paris and I'm staying at my daughter's for the moment. I'm divorced and . . ."

She stopped me with a gesture. She had delicate fingers, no rings, only a small gold chain at her wrist.

"It's more fun to guess. You're about thirty." It was more an affirmation than a question.

"No."

"How old then?"

"Forty-two."

I'm a petty liar. I should have told the truth or ripped off fifteen years. Instead, I deducted a paltry three.

"I wouldn't have thought so. You have a young voice."

That put new heart into me.

She took a package of Gitanes and some matches from her pocket. Automatically, my hand flew to the lighter in my pocket, but I stopped in time.

She lit her cigarette, inhaled deeply, then leaned back in her chair. "Do you have a mustache?"

"Do I sound like the kind of man who'd have a mustache?"

"I don't know. Perhaps."

I took out a Gauloise. "All right, yes, I do have a

mustache, I'm tall, tanned, my ears don't lie flat, I played in *Gone with the Wind* and my first name is Clark. Who am I?"

Suddenly she pointed her cigarette at me as if it were a pistol. "You're smoking. When I took out my cigarette you didn't offer to light it for me. Why?"

From the very beginning when we first began to talk I was filled with self-confidence, sure that I would say the right things, tell her what she wanted to hear.

"I prefer to light my own cigarettes and I thought you might too. Besides, you carry matches, you manage very well without any help."

She said nothing. With her thumbnail she tapped the tip of her cigarette. The ash landed neatly in the ashtray. She must have discovered the ashtray earlier, unobtrusively, with her free hand, remembered exactly where it was on the table, and click! she hit it on the nose. She's wonderful!

"My name is Laura Bérien. I'm blind, as you know, I live in Paris, I'm thirty-four, I have one sister and a white cane. And I get gentlemen I meet in the movies to offer me glasses of beer."

She had a very pure profile. There was something about the line of her neck that made me want to sweep her up, throw her over my saddle and gallop across Dakota, Wyoming, Arizona to the ranch of our dreams, where we'd live to the end of our days, divinely happy amid kisses, chirping birds, summer blossoms, heavy blankets of snow and tame Indians. Careful, Bernier, you've passed the age of adolescent love affairs.

She put out her cigarette. "I wonder what happened to Tordo. I've always had a weakness for monsters, I hope they didn't kill him."

"No, Teresa fell in love with him, they got married and had lots of little monsters."

She pushed back her glass, put her elbows on the table

and rested her chin on her hands. She was dreaming for
a moment.

"What did Teresa look like?"

"A girl, two eyes, a nose, a mouth—there must be
millions with a face just like hers."

With the tips of her fingers she stroked her cheeks,
then turned to me her words coming slower now: "At
first I was afraid I wouldn't remember what mine looked
like."

I gazed at her. She looked even more beautiful than
before. I knew I must let her talk.

"It's strange to exist and yet not know what you look
like."

There was a moment of silence. Don't be sad, Laura. I
don't want you to be sad. I knew then that I must sum-
mon the courage to tell her what I wanted her to know.

"Even if you can't remember, that's all right, because
I know. And I can assure you that you don't look at all
like Teresa."

She put her head back a little. I went on: "How did it
happen?"

She shrugged. "Medical terms are so complicated—
an extremely rare case of eye disease, apparently. To put
it briefly, a gradual weakening of the optic nerve. For
a few months the light grew dimmer and then suddenly,
click! it was turned off. A very bad joke."

It was warmer now and crowds of people filled the
streets. You could hear the voices of bathers in the distance.

"Did it happen a long time ago?"

"Four years." She sat up straight and put her hands
on her knees. Suddenly she smiled again. "And I still
don't know whether or not you have a mustache."

"No, I don't have a mustache. But I have green eyes, a
blood-splattered snout, a hairy face, I'm thirty feet tall
and my name is Tordo."

She laughed, her eyes focused squarely on my face. I suddenly thought: she has lied to me, she can see me, the whole thing's a hoax. I felt such a large lump in my throat I thought I was going to choke.

"Will you tell me the time, Tordo?"

Good lord! I had forgotten! It was almost five.

I slipped a ten-franc note under the cork coaster. Come along, Bernier, your holiday will end early this year. It was brief, but you'll never forget it. If you leave without uttering her name, you'll never recover.

"It's about five, Laura. I'll take you back. Will you hold my arm, or would you rather . . ." What? I myself didn't know.

She stood up. "We'll walk arm in arm. After all, you don't have to be blind to walk that way."

The shirt fabric above her elbow felt soft and fresh. We strolled down the boulevard.

"She'll be waiting for me in front of the Casino. She's driving a navy-blue Citroën. The right front fender has a dent in it."

The light turned green. We had to cross.

"Would it bother you if your sister saw me with you? I can leave you quite close, if you prefer. You would just have to walk a few feet and you'd be in front of the Casino."

The wind blew a curl against her cheek as she shook her head. "No, it doesn't matter. But you're a very sensitive monster."

We were there. Her hair had a lemon scent, well, not precisely—yes, it was lemon—I wanted to remember it exactly.

I let go of her. The palm of my hand retained the feel of her softly rounded arm.

"Here we are."

With a boyish gesture, she shoved her hands into her

pockets. At that very instant I saw the car turn the corner. I had twenty seconds left.

"Listen, Laura, I have two confessions to make: I'm not really thirty feet tall, and I want to see you again."

"See you"—that was clumsy of me, words that had no meaning for her.

She lowered her head. All I could see was the blond of her hair. Then suddenly she smiled. Behind us I heard the sound of a car door opening an shutting. She was about to go. I had waited until it was too late. Farewell, Laura.

Then, as naturally as if she were asking me to pass the salt, she said, "Come by some afternoon, Villa Caprizzi, on the Gorbio road."

The sister put her arm around Laura and embraced her, but her eyes were focused on me. She didn't resemble Laura at all, her chin seemed somewhat flabby and there was something forbidding about the lines of her mouth. She looked at me suspiciously, like a dowager at the opera. If Laura should ask what I looked like, she wouldn't paint a flattering picture.

Laura introduced us. "My sister Edith. This is Tordo, the monster from the beyond."

Somewhat taken aback, Edith murmured, "Very happy to meet you," but her heart wasn't in it, she didn't seem sure that Laura was joking. Only the two of us laughed. Then, after they had started off, I watched the car disappear around the corner, convinced that I would stay here, glued to the spot until the end of time—or at least until the new school term began.

In a burst of joy, the light of the sun was abruptly turned on full voltage, and I saw birds, scarcely flapping their wings, shoot straight upward like arrows. Above the gardens they veered in their flight and headed directly for the mountains, for the sun.

Back at home I found only Max and Kim. The spaghetti was boiling merrily. Singing at the top of my lungs, I set the table. It was then I remembered I had left my books at the movies.

I also realized that nothing could have bothered me less.

# *Laura*

*I*MPOSSIBLE to sleep, although tonight all is quiet on the other side of the wall. Apparently the younger generation is far less passionate than I'd thought—no staying power.

I still can't realize what has happened to me. I, Jacques Bernier, go on vacation in the Midi July first and fall madly in love three days later, after a good twenty years of emotional serenity.

During that time I had had affairs, of course, but nothing like this—not even with Stéphanie. I had met her at a convention of secondary schoolteachers. After three days of utter boredom, we had spent the fourth in a hotel room just to break the monotony. Developing into a pleasant habit, the affair had lasted three years. It had probably died a natural death long before I realized it was over.

The dark is all around me but for a single moon ray, its pale rapier-like light piercing a slit in the shutters, stabbing the floor at the foot of my bed.

Laura . . .

I'll go there tomorrow, of course. I'm not going to wait, to pretend I'm busy, that I have a lot of people to see: "I'm sorry, I would have come sooner but some old friends at Saint-Paul-de-Vence detained me." No, I would have behaved that way at eighteen but thank goodness I've grown up a bit. Besides, how could I bear to spend the afternoon in the hills, trudging on the chalky roads, knowing she was expecting me at the villa—alone, in permanent darkness? And what if she might become a little less blind if I were close to her?

But is she really waiting for me? She may have friends or all sorts of other preoccupations. I might go there to find her living room full of people—fops, old ladies pouring tea, people who play the piano or the harpsichord, and Laura in the center of the room, greeting me with a smile. "Come and meet my friends. This is Jacques Bernier, professional seducer, he tried to rape me at the movies."

All those people crowd around me. Their faces, resembling Tordo, terrifying! Suddenly they all pounce on me. I shriek frantically an clutch my pillow.

Damn! Just as I was dropping off I had to have this nightmare.

Laura . . . Blind is a word whose meaning I don't grasp. What do you see when you don't see anything?

And another question: is it possible to be desirable, to be loved, if you can't be seen?

Alone in my bed I have to laugh. I who have always loathed being conspicuous, I who have always wanted to slip by unnoticed, I've really found the answer: I love a woman who can't see me.

The moon's rays had disappeared, but the room was much lighter. Dawn was breaking.


"What was the matter with you last night? You screamed out as if your throat were being cut."

I looked at Anne. She was arranging flowers. A thorn

of the rose bush had pricked her finger and she was sucking it.

"I had a nightmare."

She scowled at me. "You look so fancied up, all shaved and shiny. Are you going out again?"

"Yes. If you're planning to hire a tail to follow me, better choose a real smart one."

Françoise was wearing a bikini that could fit into the palm of my hand. Seated cross-legged on a wicker chair on the terrace, she was covered with a yellowish cream that gave off an antiseptic odor.

"I bet your father is breaking hearts right and left in Menton."

Rubbing his scalp, Frédéric looked up from his newspaper. "What's she like?"

What finally got me was that they didn't believe a word of it. They were teasing me gently, thoroughly convinced that an old dodderer like me didn't have a chance with the opposite sex, that such things had ended for me a long time ago. I played along in the hope they would leave me to my own devices.

"She's eight and a half, has long pigtails, and gives me all her caramels."

Françoise chuckled and one of the Christs, who was arranging a pile of records on the book shelf, stopped for a minute.

"Right on! I've always said that difference in age is just an illusion deliberately fostered by the bourgeoisie to prevent children from learning about love."

"You may think so," Anne intervened, "but that's because you're a leftist."

Jesus spun around. "You're wrong," he protested. "I merely claim that children experience sexuality and that society is determined to repress it. So your father's little girl is lucky to meet an adult who is both affectionate and sensual."

Françoise stretched out her interminably long and grease-smeared legs. "Completely loco, that hombre."

Anne laughed and Frédéric concluded: "In any case, if you're not back by tonight we'll call the vice squad."

All this was tiresome, but I had only myself to blame. Before I stood up to go, I added: "Okay, look for me in the cell for dangerous molesters."

Kim, wearing an old battered hat to shield her face from the sun, entered at this point. "In any case, if you're going into town, would you mind picking up some sugar and coffee? We're all out of both."

Frédéric threw up his hands, tossing the paper aside. "For God's sake, Monsieur Bernier has better things to do than run your boring errands."

"But they're for tomorrow night," Kim protested. "If we're going to have a party we'll need . . ."

It was true, I had forgotten all about it. They were planning a party to end all parties—supper out in the open over a bonfire, music, singing—a real hippie festival, just what I need to make me feel at home!

"Okay, Kim." I was leaving. "I'll remember the sugar and coffee."

As I was about to take off, Anne shouted: "Don't get yourself kidnaped. We're expecting you for dinner."

I waved and drove off. The address was buzzing in my head: "Villa Caprizzi, on the Gorbio road."


"A glass of beer."

"Make it two."

Laura smiled as the waiter walked away. "Well, what did you tell them?"

"I don't remember exactly; that I had a date with an eight-year-old girl with pigtails, or something like that."

Part of her was in the shade. She moved her chair slightly to get all of the sun.

"How old is your daughter?"

"Anne was twenty-four last October. She has lots of good qualities, especially a talent for surrounding herself with odd characters and then delivering me into their hands."

She was wearing a plum-colored sweater and the same blue jeans she had worn yesterday. Sneakers replaced her espadrilles. Going to see her had proved childishly simple. I had rung at her gate. She had opened it after descending the porch steps like a ballet dancer, then stood on her side of the gate.

"I've come to treat you to another glass of beer," I said.

She answered gravely, "No, today it's my turn." Turning around, she called, "Edith, I'm going out."

Without waiting for an answer, she came through the gate and in a moment we were side by side in my car.

With the tips of her fingers she touched the windshield, felt the steering wheel and said: "I like three-horsepower Citroëns."

I whistled with admiration, we laughed, and now we were on the terrace of the Continental café. All around us, families were eating multicolored ice creams topped with swirls of whipped cream.

I had been talking to her ever since. I noticed one thing: my hands were trembling and I couldn't seem to control them.

She was toying with her glass. "You know, a funny thing happened to me last year at this café. Edith was at the hairdresser's and I was waiting for her here, at a table. Suddenly I heard someone sit down next to me and a voice asked: 'How about taking a ride?' I was dumfounded! I asked the man what right he had to think I would go for a ride with him. He said, 'Because you've been staring at me for the last ten minutes.' "

Her laughter was infectious.

"Ever since then, whenever I go out, I keep shifting

my eyes from time to time to avoid that kind of thing."

There was a silence.

Very quietly, I moved my chair a few inches around the table. Her eyes, still focused on me, followed.

"Magnificent! I must confess that yesterday I thought you were pulling my leg."

She seemed delighted and I of course rejoiced in her pleasure.

"Really? I'm so glad! I can orient myself fairly accurately through sound. I've turned into a radar system, all by myself."

I took a long gulp of beer. "I have to tell you, I slept badly last night. When I woke up, I thought of those stupid movies where you see a woman in a hospital with bandages all around her head . . . A seductive surgeon arrives, unwraps the bandages, you see a close-up of the surgeon looking very anxious, little by little her eyes begin to focus, then she shouts, 'I can see, Alfred, I can see!' and a half gallon of tears runs down her cheeks."

"I must have seen the same movie. It's the kind that's always a big box-office hit."

"I know it's idiotic, but I imagined that I was the surgeon, which makes it even more stupid."

Glancing away, she gazed over my head. It was hard for me to realize that she was doing so inadvertently.

"You're very nice, doctor, to dream about such things."

I placed the tip of a Gauloise on the back of her hand. She took it, put it in her mouth, and I leaned over to light it. She puffed just as the flame touched the cigarette. I think she must be guided by the sensation of heat.

"I'm sorry to disappoint you, my dear Alfred, but actually the movie doesn't end that way. No miraculous operation is possible; I'm stuck with the way I am. Are you disappointed?"

I took a long puff of my cigarette. "It doesn't disappoint me—on the contrary, it suits me just fine. You

know the Charlie Chaplin film: the blind woman recovers
her sight and thinks Charlie's so homely that she doesn't
even recognize him. If you had to undergo such an operation, I'd pray heaven that it would fail."

Removing a bit of tobacco that had stuck to her upper
lip, she said quietly: "That's mean! Besides, you under-
estimate yourself. Edith gave me a rather flattering description of you."

That literally took my breath away! "You'll have to
excuse me for a few minutes. I'm going to send her a
truckful of roses."

Laura laughed. "Wait a minute. Let's not exaggerate.
She didn't say you resembled Clark Gable. But you
didn't look like Tordo either."

I chuckled. "So good of her. She'll have to make do
with the flowers in her garden."

She pushed back her chair. "Anyway, did it ever occur
to you that when a woman is sightless a man's looks no
longer matter in quite the same way?"

I suddenly felt stupid. I often do but now I felt it
with a special intensity.

Laura was silent but seemed content. She moved her
arm to the back of her chair. I noticed her white bra
strap, the curl against her cheek.

Then suddenly I saw them on the sidewalk, a few feet
away. I spotted Françoise first because her head rose
above the crowd like a submarine's periscope. She was
eating an ice cream cone.

I leaned toward Laura. "We've got company."

She smiled and said nothing.

Anne was the first to see me. She looked at Laura and
registered surprise. Obviously she thought her old man
was doing rather well for himself. Licking her ice cream
cone, she stopped in her tracks. Françoise, plainly consumed with curiosity, nevertheless held back.

Anne's reactions are quick. Although her work is in

television, she has a good sense of theater and an instinctive feeling for complicated situations.

"Should I keep on walking as if I didn't see you? Or may I come over and say hello to my beloved Papa like a proper daughter?"

I was rather proud of her—a feeling I often have. "Laura, I'd like you to meet my daughter Anne. Right now she's dying of curiosity. And this is her friend, Françoise."

Laura was the first to hold out her hand. Both girls shook it. The gesture was so natural that neither one caught on. "So glad to meet you. As you can see, I've grown quite a bit since yesterday."

Anne bit into the cone with relish. Sometimes she seems still a child just out of school. "That's right," she answered. "Imagine, he told us he had a date with an eight-year-old!"

"Eight and a half," I interrupted, "don't make me a bigger liar than I am."

"Sit down and join us," Laura said, extending her arm.

Anne and Françoise exchanged hesitant glances. "No," Anne said, "I'd like to but we've got lots of things to buy. We're having a party tomorrow night and . . ." Frowning, she appeared to be deep in thought. "In fact," she added, "we'd be awfully pleased if you would join us. It's just a little get-together, a housewarming, and . . ." She was off in her usual avalanche of words and wouldn't stop until she'd persuaded Laura to come.

". . . and the truth is, my darling father is horribly bored with us. I'm so glad he knows you because I realize it's not much fun for him just with us."

Before I could protest, Laura raised her hand for a chance to speak, as you do in school. Anne suddenly stopped talking. Laura had managed to silence my daughter, a feat I had never accomplished in twenty-four years.

"Of course, I'll be happy to accept. It's really very nice of you but I want to warn you about something, although maybe you've already noticed. I'm blind."

Anne stopped licking her cone and stared. Françoise's jaw dropped.

"Well, no," Anne said, "I hadn't noticed."

Laura laughed very lightly. "Then I was right to alert you."

Suddenly Anne seemed at a loss. She looked at me, then back at Laura, and stammered: "But I don't see . . . well, I guess it makes no difference if, but . . . Oh! I'm sorry, I don't know what I'm saying."

Paternal feelings stirred in me and I hastened to her rescue. "Don't worry, my girl, Laura promised you she'd come. Now run off and do your shopping."

Laura held out her hand. Anne grasped it with a sigh of relief. She was still in a state of shock. She kissed me, turned to go, came back, and finally murmured. "See you tomorrow night." Françoise had already disappeared. The two of us were alone again.

"Does it bother you?" Laura's fingers were twisting a curl and there was a hint of anxiety in her voice.

"What?"

"That your daughter knows you're taking advantage of a woman who can't see and trying to seduce her?"

"I'm not trying to seduce you."

She laughed. "You've been doing nothing else."

"Me? Now that's too much! I offered you a glass of beer yesterday because I was thirsty, and I came to fetch you today hoping you'd do the same for me, that's all."

"Okay. Okay. We won't talk about it. But seriously, would it bother you if I came tomorrow night? I didn't ask you how you felt about it."

Her hand lay on the table and I squeezed it. She left it there and neither of us moved. A tune was running

through my head that very minute, a throbbing rhythm
I didn't recognize, but I knew the melody was prompted
by you, Laura, only by you.

# Geronimo

*I* had always thought that real happiness could be found only in movies, that everything worked out wonderfully only in films, where at a given moment the hero happened to be in a certain place, a villa bathed in moonlight, a small candle-lit restaurant with gypsy music playing, or a party at the opera with people dancing under crystal chandeliers. There are specialists for this sort of thing, screenwriters who dream up happy endings.

But this time I myself was in the movie, a wide-screen production in brilliant technicolor.

The flames changed Laura's golden hair to copper, Françoise was laughing in the shadows of the fig tree. Then everything grew quiet and night fell, with only the dry branches crackling in the fire.

The bottle tilted, the ruby wine glistened as the glass was filled.

"Laura . . ."

She lifted her glass and drank.

I gazed at her. Her head was flung back, her eyes reflecting the stars that were everywhere tonight, suspended above the hills. There was a throb of the guitar against the low wall, then the notes fell as slowly as warm, intermittent rain.

She leaned toward me. "All this reminds me of a Western."

"In a while you'll be seeing the Comanche Indians. They have us surrounded. Geronimo is their leader."

In the night her laughter was softer than in the day; our shoulders touched. One of the Christs was playing. His dark, husky profile seemed part of the taut canvas of the sky. Kim was dancing.

We were all spread out in a large circle around the fire. From time to time Max would go over to stir it; the palms of his hands were covered with blood-stained scratches. The flames rose, the wood crackled and exploded. Franz's glasses glittered now and then as he sat, motionless.

Anne and Frédéric were whispering. Something told me they were talking about us, but I didn't care. Tonight I didn't care about anything. It was a postcard evening, the Mediterranean night that travel agents promise you, with the scent of thyme, stars studding the sky, and the steadfast dance of the planets stretching from one end of the horizon to the other.

For their campsite they had chosen a spot rather high on the mountain, and we had walked single file along a goat's path with Françoise in the lead like a general, a bottle of vodka clutched in each hand. Max stumbled on stones. There was good reason for that. He had dipped into the wine bottles before anyone else, and besides he was carrying a huge bag crammed with sandwiches.

Laura chatted as she climbed. I held her arm and the wind wrapped her long skirt around her legs. She was in excellent form, had shaken hands with everyone and made quite an impression on Virgil, who talked to her at length about dodecaphonic music. We all drank a glass of dry rosé, then, wanderers in the night, we started to scale the heights above the village.

At a bend in the road we came upon the lighted bonfire.

Laura took a deep breath. "Grilled lamb. It smells good."

It was all very gay. I had appropriated a bottle of wine for the two of us, but it wasn't enough. Predictably, Anne urged me to recite a scene from *Le Cid*, taking all the parts at once. Whenever there is company she does that within the first ten minutes. I put up a battle but Laura added her pleas to the chorus. Maybe it was the wine I had drunk, but I thought I detected a note of tenderness in her voice. That moved me. I threw myself in to the parts:

> *". . . See, my head*
> *Is bowed before thee; do thou avenge thyself."*

I played Chimène, Roderick, the King, the Infanta and brought down the house! Laura applauded like mad. Somewhat embarrassed, I drank from her glass. Then Antoine's woolly head popped up out of nowhere in the darkness. He was offering me a lit cigarette.

"Does this tempt you?"

I recognized the odor of hash. Anne used to smoke it and her studio had reeked with the stench of burning cord. To my relief, she had stopped, claiming it made her nauseous. She had admitted to me that it never "sent" her and that she was tired of simulating an ecstasy she could never achieve. One fine day she had chucked her Katmandu pipe out the window.

That kind of thing frightens me. I've never been able to quit smoking for more than two weeks at a time. If I took up drugs, I would surely be hooked and locked up as an addict in a clinic for incurables.

I refused politely and turned to Laura. "Antoine is offering you a drag."

She turned him down with a smile and Antoine stole away like a conspirator.

Laura sat with her head thrust back, her arms hugging her knees. "What about you? Have you ever tried it?"

"I never smoke hash. I prefer main-lining."

Max was dancing with Kim, their silhouettes black and red.

"Everything is suddenly so quiet. What are they doing?" she murmured.

This was the first time she had asked such a question. It was sweet to me, but also painful. I forget when I'm with her that she's blind.

"The fire is dying, Max and Kim are dancing, Virgil is playing the guitar. I can't see the others. Anne and Frédéric seem to be asleep. Françoise has disappeared. The day is about to dawn."

"And Geronimo hasn't attacked."

She was seized with a sudden shiver, my hand touched her cheek as I draped my jacket over her shoulders.

"Thank you."

The party was over. It had been merry and glowing, but now the fire was dying. They would sleep here on blankets and Virgil would go on playing softly until dawn.

"Shall we go?"

Her eyelashes cast shadows on her cheeks yet her face was alight.

"All right. But I'd like to walk."

We stood up together. Anne saw us and came over, her shadow on the rocks flickering and distorted.

"Are you leaving?"

"Yes," said Laura. "I've had a marvelous evening! And I'm not just being polite when I say that."

Anne beamed. It was lighter now, and I could distinguish the blue of her shirt.

"I'm so happy! You're sure you weren't bored?"

Anne loves to have company but, strangely enough,

for the first time I felt that she wasn't merely being courteous, but rather that she hoped with all her heart that Laura spoke the truth.

Laura put her hands on Anne's shoulders. "I've laughed so much, I've drunk so much, and thanks to you, I feel very happy. Please believe me."

We walked down the path and I didn't turn back even though I knew that Anne, like a troubled little sentinel, was watching us, standing erect in the first light of day, while behind her, the last wisps of smoke rose and the ashes crumbled.

The sound of the guitar had long since died away. A tiny trickle ran over the stones of a nearby fountain. Long ago, peasants had built the lip of a well, but it was gradually disappearing under a heavy blanket of moss and plants rooted in the fragmented rocks.

I guided Laura's hand and the water ran over her fingers. She knelt and drank, her lips touching the moist weeds. In the faint light, a drop glistened, ran down her chin and neck.

I was no longer afraid, and that astounded me. The palm of my hand stroked her cheek; under the curls her neck seemed fragile. I kissed her; this was happening to me, me, Jacques Bernier, the man nothing ever happens to! My jacket slid from her shoulders and I felt her arms around my neck.

She wasn't trembling; what gripped her was something else, a remote, gentle fluttering that took hold of me too. A few feet away the water was trickling. She drew away. Not knowing what to say, I just held her close.

"Take off your glasses."

I obeyed.

Her hands were on my face, feeling, touching. I'm in for it, she'll see me now and I'm scared! I hardly dared to breathe.

There, it was over. Now she knew. I cleared my throat. "Well, will I do?"

"On the whole you seem okay, though I don't know the color of your eyes, your hair." She laughed and her fingers returned to my face but this time there was tenderness in her gesture. My heart swelled. I felt enormously alive.

"Laura, I have an idea. I'll take you home. Pack your bag, I'll pack mine and we'll take off."

Her index finger still followed the contour of my lips. "I . . . listen, I must . . ."

I kissed her again. I was beside myself. Forty-five years of daily routine and suddenly Life with a capital L! This time I wouldn't let her escape. I'd hold her so close that there wouldn't be the slightest room for misfortune to slip between us.

"Say yes or I'll toss you over the ravine."

"All right. Let's go." Her hair blew about my shoulders. "What will Anne say?"

"I don't give a damn. What will Edith say?"

"She'll understand. I'll explain to her. Anyway, it doesn't matter."

The day was dawning as we drove off. I sat at the wheel not noticing what I was doing, my arms as tense as any racing driver's although I was only going about fifteen. I sensed that she was very calm, very relaxed.

"What are you thinking of?"

"The first girl I ever kissed. I must have been twelve. I pretended I'd gotten some dust in my eye and asked her to get it out. When she came close, bang!"

She laughed. "And afterward? How did it go?"

"Not bad, but I later let the son of our next-door neighbor take her off my hands."

There's something strange about a seaside town at dawn. No one is on the beach, waves beat against the deserted shore, melancholy chairs seem to be waiting for occupants. I stopped the car and we got out, breathing in the sea air. At the other end of the beach, the boats for hire splashed softly. The town was white, like an Arabian village. We sauntered almost to the jetty and then drove off again.

The shutters of the villa were still closed. When we reached the gate, I took her in my arms. Her lips tasted fresh and we kissed for a long time. All this was so new, almost painful. Laura leaned against the wall, breathless, her fingers gripping my arm.

"I want to tell you something . . ."

I felt she was suddenly disarmed, like a warrior laying aside his armor.

"What is it?"

She handed me my jacket and stood there without moving, very straight, her hands pressed against her body.

"I'm afraid."

"Of me?"

She gestured almost despairingly and threw her arms tightly around my neck. The whisper of her words brushed against my ear.

"It's four years since I've made love."

Oh, Laura, lovely Laura against the white stucco, pale in the morning light. I want to tell you so many things . . . But first there had to be an end to fear. I spoke with a jauntiness I did not feel.

"Are you afraid you've forgotten how?"

Her smile returned. I had won.

Go on, Bernier, be entirely frank.

"Listen, my darling, I'm almost forty-six. I made myself a bit younger the other day. And you can be sure of one thing. When we go to bed, if one of us dies of panic it will be me."

She smiled more gaily now. "We'll see who trembles the most," she said.

Satisfied that she was reassured, I left. The gate creaked,

I saw her climb the steps and disappear.

I sat at the wheel and smoked a cigarette before driving off. Suddenly overcome with fatigue, feeling the full weight of it, I stopped at a café and drank three strong cups of coffee. I wanted to mull things over, unwilling to lose even a particle of the happiness that had appeared out of nowhere. Like a man who is parched, I wanted every drop of ecstasy to slake my thirst, to nourish and sustain me.

We leave tomorrow.

# *Max*

*W*HAT will matter most is touch and smell.

I'll have to buy some sharper razor blades, the kind they advertise on television, with women going into raptures over men with cheeks as smooth as velvet. And I'll have to shave more closely. There's a spot I always miss right under my jaw; and shaving cream—mine smells like something out of a fire extinguisher. I'll find a better one.

While I'm at it, I'll buy a decent after-shave lotion. I have a bottle of the stuff some unimaginative students gave me about three years ago, but it smells strongly of aniseed, like a cheap Pernod. I'll treat myself to something more subtle, virile yet delicately scented. There should be one like that on the market.

And what about the rest?

A slight roll of fat near the hips, nothing to worry about. I'll do setting-up exercises for two weeks and it should disappear. But there's no time to lose, we're leaving in a couple of hours.

I sit naked on the bathroom floor, chilling my bottom, and try to remember the exercises our gym teacher used to put us through when I was in school.

Sit up straight, spread your legs, stretch your toes, bend

slowly to the left, rotate your torso, bent to the right, then back to the left. Come on, try a little harder, Bernier, my boy, put a little zip into it.

Between my nose and my knee there are a mere six inches. It should be easy to make contact. But somewhere near my spine there's something that's blocking me, holding me back.

Stop. Take a deep breath and go on to the next exercise. Lean on your elbows, take turns lifting each leg, heels off the floor, one-two, one-two, one-two.

I began to sing and I forgot about my tired muscles:

> *Aime-moi, aime-moi*
> *Quand je suis dans tes bras*
> *Je dis: Oh! la la la la . . .*

I was busy giving my legs a workout and singing at the top of my lungs when a violent thump jarred the door.

A voice shouted: "Are you coming out soon or should I come back this afternoon?"

I dove into my bathrobe, wrapping it around tightly. Then, doing my best to look dignified, I emerged.

Max was sitting in front of the door. He shoved his fist in my face to show his wrist watch, a huge waterproof affair with a face the size of a grandfather clock.

"Twenty-seven minutes," he informed me. "I've been waiting here for twenty-seven minutes!"

I was truly surprised. "Time goes quickly. You're right. Give or take a few minutes, I've been in there for half an hour." He got up with an effort, grinned darkly and entered the bathroom, dragging his feet. Before closing the door, he called out: "Are you really leaving?"

"Yes, in a little while."

"Well, then I'll say goodbye."

We shook hands. Max has a nice face, like a bear's. I like him a lot; we might have become friends. "Goodbye, Max. When you send out invitations for your exhibit, don't forget me. I'd like to see what it looks like."

His eyes brightened, but a look that seemed almost sad suddenly came into them. "Sure, but if I'd known you were interested we could have talked a bit."

"That's the way it always is, Max. You get to know people when it's too late."

He closed the door and I shut my suitcase.

I've known these young people for only a very short time but I'm sorry to be leaving them. At first, they terrified me. Now I like them a lot. You have to overlook their histrionics, their language, their general behavior. Underneath, they're very simple people, probably simpler and a good bit more natural than I am.

Without a sound, Anne had come in. She was sitting on my bed, looking at me. "Are you going off with Laura?"

"Yes."

Her hand was busy smoothing the bedspread. She sighed.

"Something the matter?"

She smiled, a little uneasily. "No, nothing's really the matter. You're a full-grown man, you must know what you're doing, but . . ."

"But what?"

"I wonder how the whole thing will end."

"I have no idea since it hasn't even started."

Lowering her head, she continued to stroke the bedspread. What bothered me more than anything else was her silence. When Anne doesn't talk it's because she's worried.

I sat down next to her. "Listen, Anne, it's all very simple. Your beloved father is deserting his daughter and going off with a woman. Is that so terrible?"

She seemed deep in thought. "Well, it could be."

"Why? Don't tell me you're jealous! Haven't you gotten over your Oedipus complex?"

She shook her head. "No, that's not it. It's just that there's one thing that doesn't seem to worry you, and I hate to bring it up. Remember, Laura is blind."

I went over to the window and leaned out. The crickets were making such a racket I was afraid she wouldn't be able to hear me.

"Sure, Laura is blind. So what?"

She too got up and came over to the window. "So nothing. Forget what I've said, it's not important. Where are you going?"

"I haven't the faintest idea. All I know is that we're leaving."

She retreated a little and looked at me, like a mother hen, with a mixture of pride, tenderness and anxiety. "Actually, beneath your placid, venerable exterior, you're quite a guy!"

"I admit I'm extraordinary. I never told you, but I'm the illegitimate son of Mata Hari."

I kissed her. It was time to leave. I was to be at the Villa Caprizzi in twenty-five minutes.

We went down the stairs together. The house was empty. "Tell them all goodbye for me."

"I will."

Outside the sun was burning. As I got in the car, Anne's face appeared at the window. "You're not going to get married, are you?"

I laughed and she laughed too. "I promise to do nothing without your permission."

The motor turned over. Anne shouted above the noise: "That's the first time you've driven off without griping about your battery!"

She was right. I hadn't even thought about it. "My dear child, if I have any trouble with the battery, I'll stop at a garage and buy a new one. Even on a teacher's modest salary, it's well within my means. I might also say that anyone who constantly gripes about his battery is an exasperating bore and I would avoid him like the plague."

Anne stood back and waved.

I put the car in first. "Ciao."

"Ciao. Bon voyage!"

She dwindled in the rearview mirror, then the curve in the road hid her from view.

There! I'd done it! My bag's in the trunk, the gas tank is full, the road ahead is wide and clear. In fifteen minutes Laura will be at my side.

Suddenly I am twenty years old.

# Émile

"BRING us two Ricards and two tomato salads, and . . ."

The corners of the patron's mouth turned down and a tragic look came over his frowning face. I thought he was going to announce the demise of his wife and children.

"I haven't any more tomato salad."

Laura was toying with her fork. "That's all right. I'll have melon instead."

The man was about to collapse. "I haven't any more melon."

I glanced at the menu. "That's really bad luck, but never mind, we'll have some eggs mimosa."

In total despair, his voice choking, he mumbled, "I haven't any more eggs mimosa."

Laura began to laugh. The man raised his arms in a hopeless gesture. "What can I do? You came so late! It's almost three o'clock. I have to provide for my paying guests. But if you stay over this evening, I can serve you anything you want."

"All right. What have you left?"

He seemed reassured. "You see, this is our day for sauerkraut. If you'd like to have some . . ."

Laura burst out laughing. The man turned to her,

astonished at her good humor. "I know it isn't a dish that's often served around here, but what can you expect? My wife is Alsatian, she can't help herself. Even when it's eighty in the shade, Wednesday is the day for sauerkraut, and we never miss. I'm used to it—we've been doing it for seventeen years—but I can understand your surprise."

I squeezed Laura's arm. "Shall we go ahead and order it?"

"Okay, but it would be nice if we could have the Ricard right away. I'm absolutely parched."

"I'll bring it right away. But remember, in one way you're lucky. You won't often eat a sauerkraut like ours. It's got everything in it: bacon, raw sausage, cooked sausage, thin lard, fat lard—well, just about everything, the way they make it in Strasbourg. Have you ever been there?"

I was dying of thirst too but he seemed like such a nice fellow I didn't have the heart to shut him up.

"I've passed through the town but I can't say I really know it."

He went on: "My wife, of course, isn't from Strasbourg proper. She comes from a place a little south of it. I met her during the war. I was part of the army of occupation at Saarlouis and she ran the refreshment bar for the noncoms."

Laura tried discreetly to remind him of our order: "Did she serve Ricards?"

He gestured with both hands. "Ricards, white wine, vermouth—everything. In those days you could get anything. The Germans were rationed but we lived like kings. Like real kings."

"I gather you didn't die of thirst."

He laughed throatily. "Oh no, no! You can say that again. We certainly didn't die of thirst. You ever been to Saarlouis?"

"No," said Laura firmly.

Overcome by the burden of his memories, he sat down next to us. "It's a terrible town, nothing but barracks as far as the eye can see, and the country is as flat as my hand." He held out his palm. "I was a sergeant at the time and . . ."

I interrupted him. "Have a Ricard with us. This round is on me."

"That's very nice of you, but you'll have to excuse me. I'm not allowed to drink. I think I may be getting an ulcer, so the doctor is very strict. Absolutely no alcohol, he said. It was hard at first, but . . ."

I had to stop him. Hostelliere Thévenet was the name on the menu. He must be Thévenet.

"Listen, Monsieur Thévenet, it would be a nuisance for you if two dead bodies were discovered in your splendid beam-ceilinged dining room."

He gaped.

"That's what going to happen if you don't get us our drinks within ten seconds."

He clasped his hands together.

"Good lord! Here I am chattering away while you're dying of thirst! My wife often reproaches me for talking too much. Émile, she says, you never stop talking and the customers are waiting. But after all, we're not animals, are we? What does a customer want? He wants to be served, of course, but he also needs the warmth of human kindness, a friendly word, a little chat. I remember, two years ago . . ."

We finally got our Ricards. Each of us drank three of them with the sauerkraut, which had a special flavor and was pretty good after all. Then we had some cheese and a *baba au rhum*.

Laura pushed back her plate. "I can't eat another mouthful. Would it be terrible if I unbuttoned my pants at the table?"

"It's absolutely forbidden, but I'm broad-minded, I'll

give you permission. Anyway, I've already unbuttoned mine."

She leaned toward me. "Shame on you! Taking advantage of my affliction to loll about indecently."

"True. In fact this very minute I'm sitting here entirely exposed."

Her hand gripped mine. "I was sure of it! I wish I could see you. Buy me a cup of coffee."

"Two coffees, Monsieur Émile."

Émile emerged from the kitchen and started up the percolator.

She unbuckled the belt of her blue jeans and her knees touched mine under the table as she stretched her legs.

"I feel wonderfully comfortable here. Where are we?"

"I don't know exactly, but the village just below is called Callas. We must have driven five hundred kilometers. Shall we stay?"

"Let's."

Émile came up with two coffees. "Monsieur Émile, do you have a room for us?"

Wiping his hands on his apron, he nodded. "In the annex. Everything in the inn is taken. I must warn you, it's nothing fancy, but at least it's clean. If you'd like to look at it . . ."

"No, we'll take your word for it."

The coffee was piping hot and I put the cup down. The room was empty. Hardly surprising: it was almost five o'clock.

"Tell me about your work. You haven't told me a thing about it."

For a moment she toyed with the pack of Gauloises, then decided to smoke one. "Well, you see, I work for an organization which finds jobs for the handicapped. If you're a paralytic, a legless cripple, or a raving lunatic and you appear there any morning they somehow find a way to make the most of your capacities. I soon realized that with the help of a dictaphone, and a tape recorder, and various other accoustical devices, I could be trained thoroughly enough to become indispensable to the organization. What's more, it seems that questions put by blind people elicit a far higher degree of truthfulness than the conventional tests administered by a psychologist."

"You mean people don't lie to a blind person?"

"Let's say they lie less."

Actually, it does seem harder to lie to her. I don't know why, but that's the way it is.

"What kinds of questions do you ask them?"

"It varies. I specialize in work-related interpersonal relations. That sounds impressive, doesn't it?"

She pulled in her stomach, buckled her belt, and stood up. "Shall we go for a walk?"

A path led down to the village. The descent was rather steep, so I held her close, my arm around her shoulders.

Two bends in the road, and there it was. We slowed our pace as we reached the arcades. It was cool there. The women had sprinkled water in front of their doorways, leaving a scent of moisture that pervaded the narrow street. Broken stairs led to narrow passageways overlooking the hills. A dog followed us, its cold nose nuzzling Laura's hand. Long ago, these must have been fortress ramparts, but now sheets were laid out to dry on the crumbling walls.

"The tower on your right was built in 1446 by Count Hubert de Callas, who died during the Crusades of a shameful disease contracted from the wife of an infidel. Hubert's son, Edmond de Callas, the thirty-fifth to bear the name, built it in honor of a young girl of the region, Adrienne de Baulieu. Believing the structure to be a phallic symbol, she was deeply offended, and sent her four brothers to punish the insolent suitor. Thus began a war that was to cause bloodshed throughout the country for three hundred years. Your turn."

Without hesitation, Laura continued: "During the French Revolution, the first story was transformed into a bawdy house, and it is said that at night Hubert appears to haunt the battlements. Abandoned during the Restoration, the tower was visited by the Emperor after his return from the island of Elba. Upon seeing it, he murmured: 'I should have shown this to Josephine.' Restored by Viollet-le-Duc, this architecturally austere tower continues to dominate the majestic countryside all around us."

In my enthusiasm, I lifted her up and whirled her around. "You're marvelous! If we're ever out of work we can always get a job as guides. We'll make a fortune!"

"We could do better than that. You'll be the guide and I'll wait for the tourists at the exit with my white cane and a tin cup."

"You'll also have to play the harmonica, it pays better."

"I'll have to learn."

I sighed with satisfaction. "It's good to know we'll never die of hunger."

The streets widened as we approached the mall. In the square, in front of the Café des Sports, some men were playing a game of bowls. Their voices reverberated strangely, as if the leafy arcade prevented the sounds from rising.

"I'll buy you a drink at the Café des Sports. It's just opposite."

The heat had abated. It was the hour when the colors were most livid: the sky over us was a deep blue and the mountain rose like a sprinter stopped in his tracks, frozen there in the yellow splendor of the summer.

You can't see it, Laura. Colors for you are a thing of the past. The green foliage against the blue sky is no longer part of your world. But it doesn't grieve me because I know that now, as I place this cold glass in your hand, the shadows have disappeared and happiness is within reach.

The room.

She finished smoking her Gauloise while I brought up the bags. I'm scared, that's certain, but I expected it so I'm not surprised.

Laura, after several attempts, found her way to the window. She breathed in the night air and turned around: "What's the room look like?"

"It's small, white, and as clean as Émile said it would be. It looks like a hotel room."

I sank down on the bed.

Dzzzzzoiiiiiiiing!

I was still vibrating like the clapper of a church bell when Laura alarmed, cried out: "Heavens! What have you broken?"

Slowly, I recovered my aplomb. "I haven't broken anything. I merely sat down on the bed."

I lifted the mattress. There was no box spring, just some metal coils that were throbbing like a hundred harps.

"Lean on it."

Laura placed the palm of her hand in the center of the bedspread and pressed lightly.

Dzzoiiing!

When the noise finally subsided, she muttered: "It doesn't seem possible. There must be some sort of strange acoustical contraption in it."

"Let's sit down together."

Dzzzzzoiiiiiiiing!

I should have timed it. It must have taken a good minute and a half before silence returned, and I realized then that the slightest movement or change of position would again set off the infernal racket.

I looked at Laura. She began to giggle.

"This," I said, "is the nuptial chamber. When people in the village hear *dzoing*, they walk up here carrying torches to congratulate the newlyweds."

Suddenly she got up, flopped down again with all her weight and I shot up like a rocket, my ears buzzing with the din. She burst out laughing and I couldn't make out what she was saying, she spluttered so.

She wiped a tear that was running down her cheek. I was about to slide the mattress onto the floor when I heard a key turned in a lock. The sound of voices was actually so close that I wondered if invisible beings had entered the room.

"Alexandre, stop stalling and go brush your teeth."

Alexandre was whistling a popular tune. There was a sound of a suitcase being opened and the rustle of tissue paper.

Woman's voice: "I think you left your drops on the table."

Man's voice: "Oh, yes, I did! Shit!"

Woman's voice: "Don't use such language in front of the children! If you have cramps tonight, don't complain to me."

Little girl's voice: "Mama, where has you put my bath-robe?"

Man's voice: "Where *have* you put my bathrobe, how many times do I have to tell you?"

Little girl's voice: "But where is it?"

Voice of boy, his mouth full of toothpaste: "You don't need a bathrobe, it's hot."

Woman's voice: "Alexandre, don't mind your sister's business. Brush your teeth."

The sound of teeth being brushed, water running, rustling of clothes. You could even hear them breathe.

Laura whispered in my ear: "Are you sure they're not in our room?"

I felt the connecting walls. On three sides they were very thick, but on the fourth a very thin beaverboard partition had been painted over. Originally, this must have

been one large room; old Thévenet had divided it to make
two. I whispered to Laura: "Listen to what I'm going
to do."

I emitted a series of sepulchral coughs. Next door, all
noise suddenly ceased. They must have frozen.

Woman's voice, distinctly tinged with anxiety: "Is that
you coughing, Alexandre?"

Man's voice: "Why don't you leave him alone? It's
next door."

Silence. The sound of shoes falling to the floor, then:
"You can hear everything in these hotels."

Laura stepped back and sat down on the bed, releasing
the full din of the springs.

There was a moan of fear, then: "There's nothing to be
afraid of, Henriette, that was just a bed squeaking."

Masculine voice, slightly ribald: "Well, well, well,"
then a whistle.

In a lour voice, Laura called, "Have you brushed your
teeth, Alexandre?"

Prepared for any emergency, I pulled two blankets off
the bed, rolled them under my arm, grabbed Laura's hand
and dragged her out in the hall.

We just had time to hear Alexandre reply "Yes, Mama"
as we ran down the stairs and out into the night.


A deep, earthy freshness seeped through the ground,
as if coming from long subterranean passages. We were
immersed in the liquid night. No stars, nothing but our
bodies, close together. I could barely see her under the
blanket.

Her breasts were hard and round under my fingers and
the salty moisture that met my lips were tears coursing
endlessly down her cheeks.

"Laura, what's the matter?"

Her voice trembled. "I don't know. I don't think I'll
ever know."

I stretched out alongside of her and withdrew my hands. "Don't you want to?"

She suddenly sat straight up. Her back was smooth and unblemished, a silken woman.

"Yes, terribly, but I don't know what's wrong with me."

I wrapped her up in the blanket and we sat quietly, without moving or speaking for a long time, smoking our cigarettes. Then when the final light of the sun slipped into the night she turned gently toward me and smiled. I can still hear the music in her voice, the voice of a woman who had triumphed over dark and terrifying things and was emerging from a difficult battle that she had had to wage alone.

"Jacques, I think I'm all right now."

# Carmen

CHARNY, 3 kilometers.

She gritted her teeth. The needle on the speedometer showed thirty-five, wavered, went up to forty.

"I'm going to shift to third."

"Go ahead."

She let in the clutch, shifted gears, and stepped on the accelerator, everything beautifully synchronized. The steering wheel remained steady, moving only a fraction. She must have once been a perfectly marvelous driver!

Up ahead, the road curved. There was no traffic, nothing coming toward us. It should be easy to handle— a slight turn of the wheel.

"Just a little ahead, a gradual bend to the right."

She slowed down, shifting to second. The speedometer showed ten kilometers an hour. I heard her muttering: "God, God, God!"

Sweat trickled down between my shoulder blades. "It should be easy. You'll be able to tell. Careful, here it is."

She braked and I could see her knuckles turn white as she swerved slightly. But just as I was about to seize the wheel, she regained control. The road ahead was straight and clear.

"There! You've done it! We're past the curve. Bear a little to the right, that's it. You can go a little faster now. What are you thinking about?"

"I'm not thinking about anything. I keep seeing massive objects about to smash into me."

"Do you want to quit?"

"I'll drive to the next road marker."

"There's a small truck just behind us. You're well over to your right, so keep going straight ahead. It's got plenty of room to pass."

I heard her mumble: "It's really weird, the strange feeling I have."

The truck picked up speed and passed us. "Careful, now, you're bearing a little too far to the left."

She straightened out perfectly.

"We're coming to an intersection. There's nothing in sight, but you'd better slow down anyway."

The area ahead was flat as far as the eye could see. Maybe we were in the Beauce, I was never sure where that region began or ended. Anyway, it was all extremely level country.

"Okay, you can stop now. You've done your kilometer."

The marker was there, partly hidden by the tall summer grass: CHARNY, 2 KM.

She braked, shifted to neutral and hugged me. "Would you like me to drive all the way to the Porte d'Orléans?"

"If you wish."

We changed places. "How did you like it?"

"I loved it! Do you know what bothered me most?"

"The mud on the windshield."

"Don't be silly. It was the thought that you could correct my mistakes by touching the steering wheel without my knowing. But you saw how well I managed."

"Like an expert."

She looked absolutely delighted, laughing happily, and

asked for a Gauloise. "A smoke for the champion! How fast did I go?"

"Forty."

She whistled. "That's fantastic!"

I wanted to ask her if she used to be a fast driver, but a tacit understanding kept us from alluding to the past, to that time when the world was visible.

I felt great, ecstatic. Four whole days since we left, and everything had been going smoothly, not an awkward moment. We've transformed our lives into a world of laughter and love.

It was the day before yesterday when the idea came to her. All the hotels were full, we'd finally found a room after about ten tries, but we had to eat in a restaurant jammed with noisy vacationers. They all knew each other and exchanged recipes for shrimp sauce, for sunburn lotions, for ways to keep the children quiet, calling to each other across the tables. I was beginning to get a head-ache when Laura's hand, like a little serpent, snaked its way between the napkins, the salt shaker, and the bottle of rosé, to rest on mine. I leaned toward her. She had a wise and reasonable look on her face that was by now familiar.

"Listen, everyone's heading south, why don't we head in the opposite direction?"

The woman was a genius! She had hit upon just the right solution.

"You're brilliant! Tomorrow we'll drive to Paris."

We made love marvelously, and the next day we had begun the long drive back.

She yawned suddenly and stretched. "How far are we from Paris?"

"We'll be there in about two hours. We're close to Montargis. You want to sleep for a little while?"

The sun was the color of sliced apple. It would still be light when we reached the city, and I was almost sorry.

I like to drive at night with her beside me, the dashboard light faintly silhouetting her neck. Patches of fleecy sky are visible between the rows of trees. Dark massive hedges line the road, and I feel as if the car is at the bottom of the ocean, with seaweeds completely engulfing the bumpers. At this moment we are alone in the world, totally alone.

"Shall we sing?"

"Let's."

We can't go wrong, there's only one duet we both know well: it's from *Carmen*.

When she was thirteen and a half, wearing a checked apron and round white collar, knee socks and bonnet, she had sung the aria before a select audience for the Mother Superior's birthday; it was sandwiched between a nocturne by Fauré and a tea with *petits fours*.

I, more prosaically, once had a neighbor who was a retired infantry captain. He was music-mad but hard of hearing. Every morning between six and six-thirty, he would play three records, always the same ones, and always in the same order. The last record, the duet from *Carmen*, was invariably played so loudly that the aria became indelibly engraved in my memory during the four years I lived there.

Paris, 117 kilometers.

Laura's voice is rising. The darkened theater undulates like the sea. On the stage, the cardboard streets climb upward. I appear, a dragoon in a red jewel-encrusted jacket, sword clanking, resplendent military cap. There she is, a splendid dark gypsy, silhouetted against the bull fight arena.

She wants to run away with a matador, the wench! Frantically, I slap the steering wheel.

> *Carmen, il est temps encore . . .*
> *Carmen, il est temps encore . . .*

Still she defies me. No respect for the military. Her voice rises, she's singing well but I'm worried about the finale. I can't make the high notes without squeaking. She continues to sing, our arias blend marvelously, it sounds like great art, sheer ecstasy! We're singing loud enough to rupture our vocal cords:

> *Oh! ma Carmen, je t'aime encore,*
> *Oh! ma Carmen, je t'a-do-ore.*

Careful, she's now bidding me adieu. I'm about to stab her. But first I must pass a fifteen-ton trailer. Now I run my sword through her.

We give it all we've got.

On a last sustained note, she expires, falling against the curtain; I'm shifting the gears to high and breaking down in heart-rending sobs:

> *C'est moi que l'ai tuée . . .*
> *Ma Carmen, ma Carmen-en adorée . . .*

The orchestra explodes in deafening brasses, clashing cymbals and booming kettle drums. Spent, the conductor drops his baton and collapses upon the music stand. The lights go up, the audience is on its feet, and I hear the thunder of wild applause.

As the heavy folds of the purple curtain fall, we take our bows, our heads modestly lowered.

"You shouldn't smoke so much," Laura cautions. "Your voice cracks on the high notes. But never mind, we're a smash hit!"

"Yes, a real smash."

Laughing, she put her hand on my knee. After the racket we'd been making a sudden silence seemed to set in.

"I'm happy with you," she said.

The smoke of our cigarettes curled against the wind-shield. I'm not very good at expressing my feelings. In fact, sometimes it's so hard to get the words out that I end up by saying nothing at all. My words remain stuck away somewhere—in a hall closet, like old clothes . . . So I didn't tell her that I loved her.

"I'm glad you're happy with me. Since we get on so well, couldn't we continue together for a while longer?"

Her lips touched my ear, then slid toward my chin. "Yes, let's."

Through the half open window, a warm July breeze wafted gently.

The haze directly ahead of us meant we were already in Paris.

# Simon

"IT'S number seventeen, a corner building. There's a bus station just opposite."

"How do you know?"

"I once bumped into it and nearly broke my neck. Edith came to my rescue."

There was a free space a little farther on. I parked at an angle.

"Do you come to visit here often?"

"No, but I know the building."

I pulled up the hand brake, then helped her out of the car.

It was nine-thirty, we were a little late. It had taken forever for the waiter to bring me the bill. To our left, the dome of the Invalides shone in the moonlight.

"I suppose I should have brought along a bottle of something."

She shook her head and tightened her hold on my arm. "I've told you, there's always something to drink. These people are my friends, I know most of them well. There's only one who's a bastard, but I'll let you discover him on your own."

We were in the elevator. The building was old but

well built. "What floor is it on?"

"The fourth."

I closed the grillwork door. The elevator rose noise-lessly, a vertical coffin hung with red velvet and beveled mirrors. On each landing, a plaster nymph brandished an enormous cornucopia in one hand; with the other, she concealed her private parts.

Laura's last remark stuck in my mind. "It's hard to imagine that someone who's blind can be a bastard. I realize of course that it's possible, but all the same I can't get used to the idea."

She was really beautiful this evening. Paris and night-time heightened her loveliness. She was wearing a pleated white linen dress, her only jewelry a large silver ring. She had applied her make-up with extraordinary dexterity—pale blue eye shadow and warm copper-colored lipstick.

"Tell me, will there be any light up there?"

She laughed as the elevator stopped and we got out.

"Don't worry. They know you're coming, so it'll be all lit up. Even when no sighted people are expected, the lights are turned on anyway. Are you nervous?"

"A little. Should I ring?"

"Yes."

Either the man had slid along the parquet floor like a cake of soap under a shower, or else he had been standing there, waiting, with his ear glued to the door. In any case, it was opened immediately.

His eyelids were closed, not like a sleepwalker's, but tightly shut, hermetically sealed. He stood there, breathing in deeply. Maybe he was smelling us.

Laura spoke up: "Good evening, Simon."

His smile uncovered saffron-colored teeth.

"Ah! It's you, Laura, we've been expecting you. You've brought your friend, that's very nice."

I don't know how, but he knew I was there.

I shook hands with Simon, who stood back, placed

two fingers on my shoulder and literally guided me to a group of people seated in the center of a circular room.

"Here is Laura, and Jacques Bernier who has come with her."

Then the bustle began. It's always a nuisance to go around shaking hands at a party, but trying to shake the hand of someone who can't see you holding out yours is worse than performing a handspring.

There were a good dozen of them, including three women. One, very young, handed me a drink. Everyone was holding a glass. I noticed that they all moved around without the slightest trouble, but not one of them, with the exception of Simon, crossed the room diagonally. Instead, they remained close to the bare wall, walking quickly, certain of not bumping into obstacles. That was why the armchairs and hassocks had been placed in the center of the room—an arrangement especially suitable for blind people. Although quite a few wore dark glasses, it was something about their bearing that gave their affliction away. I found myself seated on a green vinyl sofa with polyester cushions.

"My name is Bloux, François Bloux."

I got up, shook the man's hand and sat down facing him. I caught a glimpse of Laura at the other end of the room, talking with Simon and three other guests.

Bloux had the stern face of an apostate priest, a constant sneer on his blade-thin lips. He informed me that after working for twenty-two years as a museum guard, he had been a patrolman at the Parc Monceau.

"What about you? What do you do?"

"I'm in education, a teacher, and . . ."

A prolonged and particularly diabolical sneer! "You can stop right there. There's no longer such a thing as education."

Categorical, Father Bloux! I took a sip of my drink

and began feebly: "To be sure, we have problems, but . . ."

"No, Monsieur, no, no!"

The others turned their heads toward us. Laura approached, her forearm extended like an Egyptian dancer. Bloux continued to hold forth. His voice had a steely quality.

"No, sir! Today nobody knows anything. Long ago our teachers knew how to educate."

A voice behind me: "But François, give Monsieur Bernier a chance to say something."

Bloux raised a stiff forefinger as if to begin a sermon. "I'm seventy-two years old, Monsieur," he solemnly announced. "In 1923, which isn't exactly yesterday, I learned the names not only of the French departments or prefectures but also of the subprefectures into which each department is divided. Here's what I remember." Taking a deep breath, he proceeded in rapid-fire fashion to name several prefectures together with their subprefectures, then added: "I'd prefer that all of you here call out the names of the departments; I'll follow up by giving the subprefectures for each of them."

I could hear an old lady murmur: "There he goes again."

Bloux was panting with impatience. He rose and began jumping up and down like a goalie ready to block the ball. "Come on, I'm ready, who'll begin?"

The very thought seemed to give him such pleasure that I hastened to comply: "The Haute-Loire?"

Bloux's response was swift and loud: "Le Puy, Brioude, Yssingeaux."

I whistled in admiration and Bloux relaxed slightly.

"The Vosges," Laura offered.

"Epinal, Neufchâteau, Saint-Dié." He ran all the names together.

I whistled again. Bloux waited a few seconds, then,

like a gladiator who had just slain his adversary, he thrust out his thin chest and in a fearsome voice shouted: "Are there any more takers?"

He hitched up his trousers, sat down and concluded: "All this just goes to prove that once upon a time teachers knew how to teach, whereas today . . ."

"Excuse me." I beat a hasty retreat, and squeezed Laura's arm.

"Everything okay?" she smiled at me.

"Yes. I've spotted the bastard."

"I knew you'd have no trouble."

"It's not hard when he makes no effort to hide his identity."

"Good evening, Laura Bérien. It's Maxime."

The man who addressed her was young and very handsome, one of the few men present who wore his hair long. I hadn't seen him until now; he must have been in an adjacent room.

"Good evening, Maxime. I would have recognized your voice, you know. I want you to meet Jacques Bernier."

He struck me more forcibly than any of the others. His pupils were white, the irises slightly veiled and almost colorless. Perhaps that's what bothered me. No one should have to be blind, but I couldn't help thinking that this applied to him especially. His gestures were slow and very graceful, almost voluptuous.

A couple passed us, the woman brushing against the wall. They made the rounds and left. There was another thing I hadn't noticed before: they all moved in the same direction, from left to right, an did so with remarkable ease.

"Oh, excuse me!" The only sighted person there, I had to be the one to bump into the little old lady. She was feeling her way by tapping her rubber-tipped cane along the carpet.

"Pardon me, I'm terribly sorry." I was leaning against

the wall, getting in everyone's way. I felt for all the world like a pedestrian lying flat on his back in the middle of the Place de l'Étoile at rush hour.

A heavy-set fellow was heading straight for me. I stepped aside and walked over to the window.

Laura was chatting with Maxime. Someone else joined them. I had stayed away from her, not wanting her to think that I couldn't let her out of my sight. Soon I'll have her all to myself again. Tonight she's on loan, because I'm so obliging.

"Monsieur Bernier . . ." It was Simon, accompanied by the young girl who had offered me a drink. "Could we talk to you for a minute? We'd like to ask you something."

"Of course."

"Monsieur Bernier, you've fallen into our trap," Simon said.

Across the room, I saw Laura and Maxime smile at each other. With his dead man's eyes, Maxime seemed to be staring at her. That fellow is quite different from the others. He scares me.

Simon's old-ivory teeth seemed pointed in my direction. "It's only a small favor," he said. "We all read Braille but some of us are voracious readers and can't get enough. In short, one purpose of these gatherings is to invite a sighted person, a friend or relative, to read aloud from a book or article chosen by our selection committee. We record each reading and hope in this way to build up a sizable collection. Would you agree to be our reader tonight?"

Although I was taken by surprise, the thought of reading to them was not at all displeasing—quite the contrary. Perhaps there was a streak of perversity in the idea that they would be dependent on me, that in every word I read I would be expressing myself for their sole benefit as someone possessed of the faculty they lacked.

"I'll be happy to, of course, but I'm not a very good reader."

"I'm sure that's not true. We'll begin shortly."

They went off, brushing against the walls. So, Mademoiselle Bérien, you've ambushed me. I'll get my revenge and it will be sweet indeed!

"Laura, may I speak to you for a minute?" Taking her arm, I steered my way among the other guests and led her to the center of the room. "Are you sure they're all blind?" I whispered.

She looked frankly astonished. "Of course I'm sure. This is a club of sorts, a very pleasant one, I might add, but its rules are quite strict: everyone except you is blind."

"Okay. Just imagine that they're all surrounding us at this very minute. Can you visualize that?"

"What are you driving at?" she asked, a trace of anxiety in her voice.

"You'll see."

I took her glass, carefully placed it on the floor, and drew her close to me. With my right hand I pulled down the zipper of her dress and caressed her back. Then I kissed her violently.

She wriggled, drew away her lips, and whispered, terrified: "Have you gone completely crazy?"

Without loosening my hold, I pushed her toward the wall, all the while murmuring like the disgraceful bastard I am: "Don't worry, they can't see us."

"Oh!" Her exclamation was muffled. Recovering quickly, she entered into the spirit of the thing and embraced me tightly. A few inches from my left elbow, a lively conversation about the stock market was in full swing. There seemed to be plutocrats among the blind too.

It was terrifying but delicious. I covered Laura's neck with kisses while Bloux, who was standing right in front of us, dolefully scratched his head.

"Stop, darling, you're smothering me."

The man next to me started when I zipped up the linen dress.

Simon called the guests to order. It was in the nick of time.

*This morning the world shines like a forgotten, unpicked fruit, like an orange in the dense foliage of an orange tree.*

Strange that they chose this text. It's all about color and light. Every time I uttered the words I felt as if I were handing a glass of clear fresh water to someone dying of thirst in the desert.

They were listening, their heads turned away, seemingly inattentive. It's difficult to grasp the fact that people can listen even when they're not looking at you.

Although she seemed to be asleep, Laura's hand toyed with a loop in the curtain. Maxime stood near her, a pale and radiant Dracula. I'm sure he spends his days hidden in the crypt of the family chateau. As for Bloux, he had left quite a while ago. The silence was broken only by my voice and by the faint sound of the tape recorder unwinding before me.

Stealthily, I turned to the last page and quickly looked at it without interrupting the reading. A hundred and sixty-five pages in all, and I was only on the forty-fifth! I'd never make it to the end. To make matters worse, no one looked tired; they all sat there as if spellbound.

*Good morning, beautiful wild rose, my companion in solitude, you have blossomed in front of my door during the night. The morning air is filled with the smell of freshly-cut grapevines and bunches of withered thornbushes . . .*

No time to sip my drink. I was chained to my book

like a convict. Independent of my reading, my mind kept working. What if I skipped a chapter, maybe two?

Or even three?

We could leave sooner. I couldn't wait to be alone with her.

The first time at her place, I had barely deposited our suitcases when she initiated me into her favorite game—the death race, she calls it.

The four rooms of her apartment have connecting doors. She began by opening all of them, returned to the entrance hall, then took off. Racing furiously through the rooms, she turned around in the last, then, elbows hugging her sides, and missing the door frames by no more than an inch, she ran back to me, hurling herself into my arms, breathless.

"What do you think of that?"

I was cold with sweat. "What would happen if there was a draft and one of the doors blew shut?"

"Guess."

"Bang!" I replied.

"Right. But so far there's never been a draft."

"You've just been lucky."

I had foolishly thought that to live with a blind person you had to be something of an attendant—a trained nurse reading aloud to the accompaniment of soft music in an atmosphere of quiet. But here I was with a maniac who specialized in racing through apartments going to science-fiction movies, and driving a car. It all goes to prove that you have to be leery of preconceived ideas.

Taking my hand, she had shown me around. The place was beautiful, full of light, very white. She had kept a few old family pieces but they were lost in the snowy white of walls and ceilings. Even the floors were painted.

"I should have brought my skis."

"Do you like it?"

"Yes."

For a moment she had stood there lost in thought. "I had everything repainted when I went blind. I couldn't stand the thought of being in a dark place, it seemed that . . ."

With her hands she outlined a circle, the tips of her fingers touching. "If it were dark outside of me it would be even darker in my mind . . . For a long time I used to go to sleep with the lights on."

Laura alone in the double night, struggling, turning on lights like a child afraid of the dark . . . There are times when I can't stand the thought.

I lifted her in my arms.

"What are you doing?"

"Guess."

When her back touched the blanket she whispered softly in my ear: "Well, young man, how's your sex life?"

I had a close-up of her smile, right there in front of my eyes, and her lips so near they shut out the room. "I can't complain. What about you, Grandma? No more sob stories?"

*The day is filled with opaque shadows. The night is transparent, like a chalice of holy water, and I circulate among corpuscles of your effervescent blood . . .*

For the last ten minutes I had been reading without understanding. Language and thought had become dissociated, and as I intoned Cendrars' text my mind was far away, in the glistening room where Laura and I made love. Sandwiches on the nightstand, ashtrays overflowing, bottles of all kinds, dishes, clothing strewn everywhere. We go out only to market, to one of the few neighborhood shops still open, on the other side of the Boulevard des Batignolles. Paris is empty, we are alone in the universe. Stretched out on the mess we've made of the bed, I can glimpse through the window the bare bones of the dead city.

Yesterday the telephone had rung. It was Simon. Assuming Laura was in Menton, where she went every year, he had called anyway, on the off chance. Delighted to find her home, he had invited her to one of the reading sessions he organized from time to time. Laura had mentioned me, with the result that here I was, reading steadily for an hour and a half.

I had just turned the page when I heard a click. It was the end of the tape.

With the sigh of a man emerging from a marvelous dream, Simon got up and turned off the recorder. His closed lids were so taut that he seemed to be looking at me with eyes made of skin.

"Thank you, that was very good of you. It's difficult to explain how much these recordings mean to me, to us . . ."

If shame could kill, I would be dead by now.

"I know you're tired," Simon went on, "so you had better stop. The book isn't finished but someone else will read the rest. Thank heavens, we have lots of friends."

What a bastard I am! Here I was, in a position to contribute something immensely important, and all I could think of was to skip pages, to play selfish, shabby tricks . . .

Everyone started to leave. As I went up to Laura, the old lady I had bumped into earlier and a gray-haired man wanted to thank me.

"You read with such delicacy . . . You expressed every nuance."

Laura dragged me off just in time to prevent me from strutting.

In the car, snuggling close to me with a sigh of contentment, she said, "Home, James."

We drove back in the warm, empty night; like other

couples, we had spent an evening with friends, and now we were homeward bound.

A couple, just another couple.

# *Paméla*

*H*EY, you guys! Cockroach is swipin' all the nails!"

Cockroach hurtled against us and I grabbed Laura, who had bumped into the fence and was covered with fresh paint from shoulder to elbow.

"Damn! Don't touch it. You've got paint on your blouse."

It was her Menton shirt, the one with patch pockets.

"A lot?"

"Plenty."

Two wooden planks fell and three small urchins emerged from behind them. The tallest, a girl with wrinkled socks and a freckled face, had a rear end as tiny as a frog's. The others, both boys, were covered with such a thick layer of filth it was hard to tell where their skin ended and their T-shirts began.

"You seen a guy runnin' away?"

"Yes, he ran into us and you can see the result."

The kids stared at Laura's sleeve. "Cockroach's the one who did it," said filthy boy number one. "He's been tryin' to hammer nails into us."

"That's right," said the girl. "He's loco, that hombre."

Somewhere I had heard the phrase before.

"Hey, Paméla, what she needs is turpentine," said filthy boy number two. "That'll do it."

"I know," Laura said, "but where do you expect me to find it?"

"We got some," offered filthy boy number one. "That's what I'm tellin' ya."

As we filed through the fence toward the construction site, I vaguely remembered reading about it in the newspapers. I even recalled the press photograph showing an excavation with barracks near the bottom of the pit, a miserable enclosure surrounded by the high walls of dark, dilapidated apartment buildings. We could hardly move without climbing over thick planks, skirting piles of galvanized sheet metal, stooping under wooden beams, and stepping all over the kids who were hammering nails with all their might, drilling, painting, throwing, shouting.

This was supposed to be one of those radical sociological experiments you hear about. I had no idea how the thing was working out but in any case these particular street urchins were having the time of their lives. This was their vacation spot, right here in the heart of the fourteenth *arrondissement*. Building cabins, taking them apart, painting fences, walls, bricks, floors—they swarmed all over the place.

Coming straight at us were two boys as thin as sticks, each at either end of a wooden plank. I shoved Laura against a plate of sheet metal, to let them go by.

Paméla, the girl in the wrinkled socks, turned around and came toward us. Her chin was as pointed as the tip of a pen knife. "Can't ya see where yer goin'?"

"No," Laura said, "I'm blind. What's your name?"

"Paméla. Give me yer hand. That man can hold yer other hand."

We walked a few steps. The two filthy boys cleared a path for us, as if they were motorcyclists riding in front of an official limousine.

"Get outa the way, ya bums, the lady's blind."

At least twenty-five of them surrounded us.

"Such is fame," Laura said.

We sat down on a pile of paving stones that seemed part of some demolished barricade.

Paméla was offering us a jug of turpentine when a bearded man shoved the crowd aside.

"No adults are allowed in here," he said.

Explaining about Cockroach and the paint, I told him that it was Paméla who had suggested coming here. His eyes softened and he gazed into the distance like a Tibetan Buddha.

"Well, that's different, if the kids invited you."

He walked off meditatively while I removed the paint with a handkerchief dipped in the turpentine.

Except for a few hammer-and-saw fanatics who continued to linger over their work, the urchins stood all around us. It was strange to be in Paris in July sitting on all this rubbish and encircled by countless children.

They looked mainly at her. A few were huddled together muttering to each other. Suddenly, one of the boys who had been standing behind us came forward. His hair glistened with tonic, his eyes were the color of prunes, and he had a bandage on every finger.

"Is it true, lady, that you can't see nothin'?"

Wiping away a drop of turpentine that trickled down her forearm, Laura settled herself comfortably before answering.

"It's true. I can't see."

A little girl in a flowered apron who was standing behind the others called out: "What about me? Can ya see me?"

I thought they were going to lynch her. A bright-eyed curly-haired kid whom they called Mohammed spun around: "She said she couldn't see, shit! If she can't see, she can't see ya, ya dummy!"

I put the turpentine away and lit a cigarette. Moham- med watched my every move; I was sure he smoked plenty himself. I handed the cigarette to Laura, who took a long puff.

"Do you want to go?"

"No, why? The seat's a little hard but otherwise it's nice here."

The children laughed and I began to question them, to give them something else to think about. "Are you really having fun here?"

"Yah."

"Yah, lots of fun."

"Yah, not bad, but gimme a beach any day."

Filthy boy number one grinned so hard the crust of dirt on his face began to crack. "I'm glad it ain't the sea. The beach stinks."

A little guy balancing himself on a plank leaned over, almost toppling. "Ya been to the sea? C'mon, tell me. I'm askin' ya, ya ever been there?"

Filthy boy number two spoke up loyally. "Ya talk big. Ever been there yerself?"

"Yep, buddy, I been there."

"Well, then?"

"Well, nothin'."

"Ya know it stinks, like I said."

"Go on, ya stupid."

Laura laughed heartily.

The children looked at her: blind, young, beautiful, and gay.

The little girl in the apron came closer. Her index finger had almost disappeared inside her left nostril.

Everyone around us was arguing. Laura blossomed, the sun shone merrily.

Placing my hand on her shoulder, I said: "You'll have to admit this is rather different from all that fancy stuff on the Riviera."

She was about to answer when finger-in-her-nose asked in a strident voice: "Well, if ya don't see, do ya see everythin' black?"

Everything stopped. Some sparrows continued to fly, the kind of Parisian birds that never venture beyond the Seine, never fly farther than the Place des Vosges.

Funny thing about kids: they can be so sensitive, so easily embarrassed. They could have killed that little girl, but the thing was done, it was too late, so they just stood there, silent, unhappy, and terribly sorry.

"No," Laura answered, "I don't see everything all black. Black is a color and I can't see colors."

She was smiling so naturally that her audience began to breathe easier. Paméla had the floor.

"Well, if everything's not black, what do ya see?"

Mohammed, offended, answered for Laura. "She's blind so she don't see nothin', why d'ya keep askin'?"

I felt Laura was relaxed and very sensitive to the children's curiosity; nor did she sense, any more than I, the slightest trace of anything morbid in their questions. These were kids from the slums, kids who didn't go off on a summer vacation; a blind person had appeared out of the blue and they were interested—it was as simple as that.

I joined in. "That's right. What do you see when you don't see anything?"

She was puffing her cigarette. "It's hard to explain. Paméla, give me your hand."

The child complied readily. The others watched in silence.

"Look at Paméla's hand," Laura began. "She can use it to touch, she knows when things are hard, when they're soft, cold or hot. But a hand doesn't see. Do you follow me?"

There was a murmur of acquiescence from the crowd. Fascinated, they listened intently to every word.

"All right," Laura went on. "You can't see with your hand, so you can't say that a hand sees black, isn't that so? Well, when you're blind it's the same thing. There is no black, there's nothing any more."

"You wanta come look at our cabin?" The girl who asked hadn't uttered a word so far; nor had anything in her attitude indicated any greater interest than that of the others. The invitation from her lips was like a gift offering.

The cabin was in one corner of the yard, near a tree that was probably the last in the neighborhood. The pathetic-looking tree was so blackened with soot that Mohammed told us he had taken a ladder and washed down the trunk with a sponge, the way grown-ups clean the Paris monuments. Why not? The Arc de Triomphe has been scrubbed, why shouldn't the tree be cleaned too? The children had built their cabin behind it but the structure was far from completed. They were thinking of building a second story, but it was tough, they said, very tough.

Laura sauntered along surrounded by kids, at least three of them clinging to each arm. I, for my part, finally handed my Gauloises to Mohammed and the bigger boys. It was pandering to them, of course, and it certainly wouldn't do their lungs any good. Okay. I knew that. But I defy anyone who meets a bunch of children spending their summer holidays in this old part of Paris—their lungs filled with the foul air of the métro and the fumes from the Seine—to do otherwise.

As we were leaving, Laura hugged and kissed at least a dozen children who accompanied us to the exit. The bearded man waved goodbye. And then we found ourselves back on the cracked sidewalk, near the bulldozers.

Beyond was Les Halles. The air shimmered in the sun above the excavation sites. Laura shook her head, apparently content but also perturbed. The turpentine on her sleeve had dried, leaving a ring.

She clutched me as a nearby pneumatic drill went into action. I had to lean over to hear what she was saying.

Our arms around each other, we walked across planks, skirted screeching power shovels, and hurried to avoid trucks piled high with gravel. Rue St. Denis was calmer and boasted a few antique shops. I read the sayings on old colored postcards, pictures in faded yellow showing soldiers with pastel-colored eyes squeezing the hands of ruddy-cheeked girls:

> *Paulette, in my heard you're my dream,*
> *In my secret thoughts you reign supreme.*

Laura loved such doggerel. We sauntered through what was left of Les Halles, narrow streets where you could still smell the odor of old cheese. She wanted some french fries. Reaching into the greasy paper bags we nibbled on them before collapsing exhausted on the chairs of a café—tiled walls and rickety tables—it was one of the last bistros that still served coffee in glasses. She was in splendid form; the children and all their questions seemed to have infused her with fresh energy.

"Where would you like to go?"

"Take me to a fancy restaurant, a really elegant one."

I looked at her. "You'll have to change your clothes. In those jeans with all that turpentine on your shirt, I'm not sure they'd even let you in to wash dishes."

"Well, buy me a mink coat."

"It's not the thing to wear in July."

"Oh, you just say that because you're a miser."

I paid for our coffee. "I'll tell you what the newspaper headlines will say: 'Seductive professor in his forties, unable to satisfy the luxurious tastes of his blond companion, crazed with sorrow, strangles her with her bra strap.' "

She giggled. " 'Seductive professor in his forties'—what

will those reporters think of next? Anyway, tonight I'll take you out. Since your modest means don't allow you to keep a woman like me in style, you can be my guest. Let's go."

We crossed the Seine as boats glided by. She liked the noise and the smell of the water. In the square of Notre Dame, a long-haired guitar player was singing the blues.

Thoughtful, Laura listened, leaning over the embankment wall. "Paris is a strange city," she said. ". . . so many places where you wouldn't think you were in a city at all."

"That's its real charm."

I felt she was growing melancholy, partly because of the American guitar player and his slow vibrating chords. As silently as possible I stepped back and stood on the other side of her. Speaking in a falsetto, I said: "Excuse me, lady, but that church over there, what is it?"

"Notre Dame," Laura answered.

"I thought Notre Dame had two towers. This one has only one. How come?"

Laura looked disconcerted. Then she pounced on me. She was laughing so much that some of her strength was dissipated, but she managed to land a few well-placed upper-cuts.

It took us a while to recuperate. I felt her lips on mine as she whispered: "You're an idiot! Your jokes are in the worst possible taste. One day you'll push me into a manhole."

"I'd already thought of it but I was saving it for later."

We walked along the quays toward the Odéon. My jacket was over my arm; Laura's hand was in mine. We had been together in Paris for eight days.

# *Bacchus*

*I*T was the Hall of Mirrors at Versailles, but less glittering, more somber.

We had scarcely taken three steps toward the damask-covered tables when at least a dozen waiters came running up, some in black, some in white, others in black and white.

A terrifying mustachioed man in tails, who looked as if he had been cast in bronze, drew back Laura's chair.

"We thought you were on vacation, Mademoiselle Bérien."

A waiter handed me a menu covered in embossed, leather, as thick as the telephone book. They knew she was blind and didn't offer her one.

"A cocktail to start with?"

Laura, very much at ease, smiled up at the paintings on the ceiling. "A Manhattan, but not too strong."

"And for Monsieur?"

I was trying to remember what they drink in whodunits. Gangsters and cops are always having fancy cocktails on every page. I had it! "I'll have a Cuba libre."

Bowing deferentially, the waiters departed.

I whistled with admiration at the chandeliers, the mirrors and the fake Gobelin tapestries. There were dusty paintings whose cracked gilt frames glistened under electric candalabra.

Laura seemed very pleased. "It's not bad, I think. I've come here with Edith a few times; she loves this kind of place. How does it strike you?"

"I've always had a weakness for museums, but I'm afraid I'll use the wrong fork. Do you want me to read you the menu? If we start now I might manage to finish before they close."

The bronze statue came back, advancing as if he were mounted on ball bearings.

"Mademoiselle, you and Monsieur have decided what you would like?"

"We're just discussing it. Can you give us any suggestions?"

He raised his eyes toward the chandeliers for inspiration, the discreet fake diamond on his ring finger sparkling as he stroked his polished cheeks. Now there was a fellow who knew how to shave!

"Permit me, Mademoiselle and Monsieur, to call to your attention our flaming oysters *á la Mornay*, a first course that our patrons always enjoy."

We discussed the menu with some acrimony. I had intended to order a good beefsteak with french fries; instead, I would have to make do with a filet mignon, some fancy kind of mushrooms, and potatoes *ducales*.

Laura was amused by my complaints. "You're trapped," she said. "This is the most chic joint in Paris and the only one where you can never order what you feel like eating. Don't ever ask for peas or green beans; they've never heard of them."

I protested woefully. "I didn't want their potatoes *ducales*! I haven't the faintest idea what they are. I just wanted french fries like we ate at Les Halles. I'm going to break his neck, that mustachioed fool!"

"*Sh,* be quiet, or I'll order some snails *á la Mont-pensier* for you. Edith had them once and she told me that about a dozen waiters cooked them right before us over a lot of little chafing dishes. This seems to be what attracts the customers."

At the next table to ours, on the other side of the statue of Diana the huntress, a trio of Dutch women had just been seated. Together they must have weighed over a ton.

Laura sipped her Manhattan and leaned toward me. "I can hear new voices," she said. "You're probably congratulating yourself again on my sad affliction. You can make eyes at any of these women as much as you please."

I choked over my glass. A waiter whose face seemed chiseled from a block of cement turned to look at me like a reproving Medusa. This was obviously no place to strangle.

"What are you laughing at?"

I put my glass down. "The best looking one resembles a pressure cooker, another is a barrel of lard, and as for the third . . ."

Laura laughed. Her fingers grasped my sleeve, crept under my jacket and stroked my arm. "Jacques, I want you to know that ever since I walked out on that movie in Menton, I haven't stopped feeling gay for a moment."

How that moved me! What she had just said meant so much—but I knew I had to keep it light, to keep my feelings from showing.

"That's because I'm such a life-of-the-party type."

She tilted her head to one side the way a mother does when she knows her child is lying. "Are you really always so full of fun?"

Poor me! A drab, dull old teacher—no duller than the next fellow, of course, but no livelier either—who lugs his briefcase from school to the métro and back year after year, drinking Dubonnet alone over piles of exam papers.

"No, I'm really not. I guess it's you who inspires me." Her fingers were still on my arm. I could see multiple reflections of her in the row of mirrors—an infinity of Lauras. "I don't have to guess, in fact. I know for sure it's because of you. Usually I'm not much fun. Some of my students probably don't think I'm at all amusing."

My filet mignon had just arrived. Inadvertently I touched the plate. It was so hot it burned my fingers. A blister was already forming when the waiter with the plaster-cast face said in sepulchral tones: "I suggest that Monsieur take care. The plates are hot." He was clearly out to get me.

Through a gap in the heavy crimson drapes, I could see the Seine, its waters cutting through the heart of the city. Laura was eating complicated and esoteric dishes with a hearty appetite.

"Is it good?"

"Taste it." She held out her fork. Little rubbery cubes covered with a pinkish sauce were on it.

Conscientiously, I chewed and swallowed. It seemed like a mixture of artichokes and chewing gum. I offered her a piece of my filet.

Mustachio and Plaster-face, their eyes heavy with disapproval, gazed at us.

Laura rested her chin on her hands. "How goes it, dear teacher?"

I was eating my potatoes *ducales*. "Great. But this kind of place always makes me want to take off my shoes. How do you explain that?"

In her best sociologist's manner, she said: "That's a characteristic manifestation of class consciousness. You're the middle-class type who registers his disapproval of upper-class conspicuous consumption by a grotesque action of highly political significance."

"What about you? Don't you ever have such impulses?"

"Sure. But I don't have the urge to remove my shoes. Maybe to perform a belly dance."

I rubbed my hands together. "I'd give a lot to see that! You want to give it a try?"

"First order dessert for me. A blueberry tart. And take my advice and try their cherries in maraschino."

"If I asked for a plain yoghurt do you think they'd call the police?"

"That's a chance you'd have to take. Pour me some wine."

Her cheeks were pink. We were on our second bottle of wine and she was blossoming.

"Afterward," she said, "we'll have some champagne."

"You're really celebrating tonight!"

"Today is my birthday."

I stared at her, feeling dreadful. "Why didn't you tell me?"

"What would you have done about it?"

"At least I would have wished you . . ."

"Well, it's not too late for that."

The table was wide. There was too much crystal between us and I was afraid of spilling something if I leaned over. So I got up, went around, took her face in my hands and kissed her. "Happy birthday, Laura."

"Thank you, darling."

Behind us the waiters must have been having fits. I went back to my seat. It's funny how that wine could affect your legs. "Waiter, if you please . . ."

A third waiter arrived, just in time for me to whisper to Laura, "Here comes a new waiter. The others have probably been rushed to the hospital."

"A blueberry tart, some cherries in maraschino, and a bottle of champagne."

He left, bowing low with respect.

"Lentils on Sunday, and the rest of the week, I gnawed

on my leather shoelaces. Yes, my dear girl, that's what my miserable childhood was like."

"Don't complain. At ten, I sold dirty postcards in the métro and my stepmother would bash me on the head to make me say thank you to buyers. So don't come to me with your stories—you had a golden youth."

I banged the table so hard the ice clanked in the silver champagne bucket. "I had to make my first communion in short pants, my sweet, because we didn't have money to buy long ones. I had dreamed for months about having a pair of long trousers."

The restaurant was empty now except for us. It must have been late, although I couldn't seem to see by my watch whether it was two-ten, or four-ten, or maybe only eleven-fifteen . . .

"At *my* communion," she crowed, "it rained all day and my rubbers ran all over my white shoes, turning them to lavender." She leaned back in her chair and let out a triumphant war whoop.

It was time to leave. I gathered up my matches, my sense of balance, and whatever remained of my lucidity. My speech gave me a little trouble; my tongue seemed to have swollen in my mouth. But after three tries, I managed to order a taxi.

We made a triumphant exit, executing a slalom between the high columns as they do at a Swiss ski resort. Then we collapsed against each other in the taxi.

Happy birthday, Laura.

# Casanova

AND three makes five, plus five, makes ten. Thank you, Monsieur."

The bright sunlight on the glass of the door hurt my eyes. My eyelids ached as I walked down the street. And every time my feet hit the pavement a gong clanged in my head.

Lucky the pharmacy was open. It's not easy to find one during the summer holiday. The aspirin and the mineral water should do her some good.

When I put her to bed, she told me the story of her life, repeating the same thing over and over. I don't think I closed my eyes all night long. She fell asleep, woke up mumbling inaudibly, went back to sleep, and was sick in the morning. We spent a good half hour sitting on the edge of the tub in the bathroom. The mirror reflected a sorry picture of a couple of drunks in the early morning light.

I held her in my arms but she couldn't stop moaning, "Jacques, I'm ashamed. I'm a drunkard."

Feebly, I protested.

"Yes, yes, I'm telling you, I'm a drunkard. I shouldn't have had so much to drink. Blind people especially ought to know how to behave themselves."

I tried to be funny. "You had no way of knowing whether or not your glass was full, so you emptied it, to be on the safe side."

"I feel as if I have two heads, one on top of the other. If I move, the one on top will fall off."

It took me a long time to calm her. When I left she was lying on the sofa, her head buried under two pillows.

Flowers. I mustn't forget flowers for her birthday. Of course the day is past, but it's not too late. I'd better buy something to eat, too. We'll probably stay in all day. If we do go out, it'll be for a short walk later on, toward the evening. Once around the square slowly, then the frail old couple will go home to their cup of tea before bedtime . . .

I finally returned with a bunch of carnations, a bottle of aspirin, two bottles of Perrier water, one Evian, a package of noodles, six eggs in a plastic box and a tin of sardines. She was up, dolefully listening to the water boiling in the coffee percolator.

When she caught the fragrance of the carnations, she ran to kiss me, then stopped short, a pained look on her face. She too had a gong beating in her head. We gulped the aspirins and washed them down with some of the fizzy mineral water.

This was perhaps our sweetest, most tender morning. Since our departure everything had been so hectic that both of us, unconsciously wanting to call a halt, welcomed this recuperative moment of rest.

I brewed tea with mint, cooked the noodles, and wished I could fix a compote of fruit. Who knows, maybe I have a hidden talent for nursing.

For a while we hardly spoke. When she asked me for a cigarette, I knew she was on the mend. As for me, I was beginning to feel a bit liverish. For years I've had trouble with my liver and you don't improve after forty. I usually watch my diet and even take a couple of pills before every meal.

Four o'clock. She was listening to Brahms, curled up on the couch, with the record-player turned low.

Why hadn't I brought my pills with me? I must have thought they would shatter our romance: Romeo kidnaps Juliet, drags her from one hotel to another all over France, gets drunk with her in fancy restaurants, carries her off in a mad whirlwind of love and folly, but never forgets to take his two liver pills. No, that's not possible.

The record ended. Getting up, Laura slipped it back into its cover. She had her own clever system of arranging the pile so that she could find the record she wanted.

She returned to the couch and lightly caressed my cheeks. "Don't you feel well?"

I made a face. "My liver's acting up."

"Have you any medicine for it?"

"No, I left my pills in Menton."

She shook her head gently. "You never told me you had any trouble of that sort. Why?"

"I often forget it myself. Besides, I don't want any shadows in the picture."

For the first time I saw her face close off. She was still there, all right, very near to me, but it seemed as if she had retreated several miles and was looking at me from the top of a hill. "What does that mean, 'any shadows in the picture'?"

Because of my liver, my headache, and my reluctance to engage in an argument, I said: "Oh, forget it! We're in no condition to discuss it."

She jumped up, and then sat down again, her legs crossed neatly, very much alive. She had obviously recovered a lot quicker than I. "Well, I don't know about you, but I'm in excellent condition to discuss it. I'm going to tell you what you're doing: you're making up a fairy tale, like a child, and you shove aside everything and anything that might cast a shadow on the picture, as you put it. But you forget one thing. There's no picture for me. Besides, we're no longer of an age to be featured on the cover of a true-romance magazine."

I knew she was right and that annoyed me. "What's all that nonsense? I'm certainly entitled to forget I'm forty-five, and you that you can't see. There's no need to make a big fuss about it."

She jumped up. "Why on earth should you have to forget it? You're forty-five and I'm blind, that's all, and we manage to get along, anyhow."

"Well, I've already forgotten about it," I mumbled.

She laughed sharply. "Well, I haven't. Sorry, old thing, but I'm always aware that I'm a handicapped person, as they put it on television, so I don't see why you, if you've got drops to take . . ."

"Pills, not drops."

"Then why don't you take your damn pills? Are you afraid I'll notice you're not a kid any more. I already have."

"You didn't notice it, I told you. That's not the same thing."

She reached out and grabbed me right on the spot where my hips have a roll of fat.

"What about that, old man, did you have it when you were eighteen?"

I drew away. "That's just because I'm sitting down. Everyone has a little roll of fat when they sit down, even you, though less than me, I'll admit."

"It's because I'm thirty-four, not because I'm sitting down. But you . . ."

"What about me?"

"Look, you are forty-five and I love you. You see, you've made me say it. But you've got to get one thing into your thick head: you haven't grown any younger just because you love me. When I go to bed with you

I know it's not a twenty-year-old who's holding me in his arms."

I was taken aback. "Now that's going a bit too far! Sure, I've got a little extra fat on me, but otherwise—well, I didn't think we were doing so badly."

She laughed. "I didn't say that, I just meant that after all . . ."

I grabbed her by the wrists and we fell to the floor. I was belting out the last aria from *Carmen* as she tried to pull my hair. She struggled but I had a firm grip on her and wasn't about to let her go.

"You're in my power, baby. I'll make you pay for this."

She kept twisting, trying to extricate herself, but was soon out of breath. "How's your liver now?" she panted.

"Don't worry about my damn liver, baby, just repeat everything I say after me or you're a dead cookie: You're a perfect, inexhaustible lover."

"Okay. You're a perfect, inexhaustible lover."

"You're an expert at making love."

"You're an expert at making love."

"Very good. Now go on: With you I've experienced utter ecstasy."

"That depends on which time." She landed a hard jab, I tried a double nelson, but she slipped away from me. To put it mildly, I wasn't exactly in top condition. Panting like a bull, I decided to call it quits.

We went out in the late afternoon and I bought a fresh supply of liver pills. I also bought some adhesive bandages—she had bashed a toe during our wrestling match. This was definitely pharmacy day for us.

We returned all calm and peaceful. My state of mind reminded me of how I used to feel as a child right after being forgiven for telling a lie. Unburdened, I could look forward to a tranquil tomorrow, my conscience altogether clear.

But I should have been leery: life sometimes turns out like a Western. When things are at their quietest, watch out! That's when danger pops up.

On the landing, in front of the door to Laura's apartment, a man was waiting. He turned a heartbreakingly handsome face toward me.

It was Maxime, and I was afraid.

He stood there eerily, as if he had suddenly materialized out of nowhere. Laura had mentioned him once or twice since the gathering at Simon's place, remarking that he loved to make unexpected appearances. I suppose it gave him a sense of superiority. That he was feeling quite pleased with himself was obvious at this moment. I was afraid to let him come in.

# *Mephisto*

*T*HE whiskey in his glass was absolutely level. The hand holding it was steady. I was glad that Laura couldn't see him—his features are so beautifully regular and classic. Ugliness consists in a lack or a surplus of bone, or flesh or skin; he hasn't a speck too much or too little. But beneath the mask of perfect poise a fire is smoldering.

Làura had been winding up her course in re-education when Maxime first joined it. He had already twice attempted suicide and had refused for a long time to learn Braille. After he'd gone blind, he had forbidden any music, even the radio, in his home. Fate having plunged him into darkness, he seemed determined to remain totally enclosed in it. For over a year he hadn't uttered a word. Then a change had come over him, and from all indications, he wanted to live again. I don't know the reason, but I suspect that Laura is part of it.

I've also learned another thing tonight: there are times when a man may feel that being sighted is a burden. That's how I felt right now.

"You're a teacher, Monsieur Bernier?"

On his perfectly chiseled lips the words seemed insignificant. What mattered was the tone. I knew that the innocent-sounding question concealed what Maxime was really thinking: What are you doing here, Bernier, among the unsighted?

"Yes, a teacher of literature."

Maxime smiled strangely. Either he makes no attempt to disguise his thoughts or else the loss of sight prevents him from controlling his facial expressions. In any case, his lips were drawn down in a look of utter contempt.

"You must forgive me, Monsieur Bernier, but educators have always struck me as lacking in imagination. You fellows enter the classroom when you're six and don't leave until you're sixty. The lot of you lead a sedentary, routine life."

Laura stirred in her chair, apparently fearful of something.

"It's true, we do lead routine lives. I leave my house every morning and return every evening. You, I know, would consider that monotonous, but I've a confession to make: adventure bores me."

He toyed with his glass and a shadow passed over his pale face, accentuating the cheekbones and giving him a gaunt look.

"You like to sound paradoxical."

"No, it's just that I consider the life of a Saint-Exupéry totally uninteresting, whereas people like airport employees whom he would probably have despised positively fascinate—"

"I have just one question, Monsieur Bernier," he interrupted. "Would you consider living with a blind person an adventure?"

The glass came down so hard on the tray that it sounded like a pistol shot.

Laura suddenly paled. "Maxime, I don't think this sort of conversation is called for. Please be good enough to . . ."

He thrust his jaw at me. "You'll quickly realize one

thing, Monsieur Bernier. In the realm of the blind, neither the one-eyed nor the sighted are kings."

He exuded an almost brutal power. My voice shook. "I don't quite understand . . ."

Laura again tried to intervene but Maxime was launched and his next words convinced me that nothing would stop him.

"A blind person, Bernier, is not merely someone who can't see, he's not a diminished person but a different one, with different ways of thinking, of feeling, of loving and hating. I can assure you of one thing: he has nothing, you hear, absolutely nothing in common with the world of sighted people. No real contact is possible."

Laura listened silently. The knuckles of her fingers turned white on the arm of the chair.

"We and you are not the same. When someone takes my arm to help me across the street, I react to him as if he inhabited another planet. Think for a minute, Bernier. Can you visualize how your face appears to me right now, while I'm talking to you?"

I stood up and lit a cigarette. "Okay, when one part of the whole changes, the whole changes too. So what?"

He raised his eyebrows and for a second his teeth glistened. "You say, so what? It's quite simple. Blind people can communicate only with each other. People like myself belong to a group apart, and no matter how hard you try, you can't get through to us. You know it, and so does Laura."

She shivered upon hearing her name. "We've already talked about this, Maxime, and you know how I feel. You're determined to break off all contact with the sighted world, to form a closed society and to . . ."

Hesitating, she shook her head violently and pushed a strand of hair away from her forehead. Then she continued: "You're too theoretical. There's Life in a large sense, and there's just plain life, which explains why I'm presently in Paris instead of Mentón, why I'm with Jacques instead of my sister. It's this life, too, that makes Jacques sighted and me blind. That's all, that's the way it is, and there's nothing anyone can do about it. As for knowing if . . . Oh, damn, let's drop the whole thing . . ."

Everything was stilled, except for the noise of a horn that echoed faintly along the street . . . Maxime slowly uncrossed his legs.

His face was blank, expressing absolutely nothing at the moment. But he went on talking as if he were reciting a text, coldly, without passion, each word falling with razor-edge sharpness.

"You're both victims of illusions traditionally entertained by the so-called political 'left.' You've probably fallen for the cream-puff stuff about mutual understanding, you believe in friendship between whites and blacks, between Jews and non-Jews, between Algerians and Frenchmen. You have a need to believe all this, yet you know that the truth is different, that every time the two races meet the word isn't Harmony but Slavery, Ghetto, Auschwitz, War and Torture. Well, if a difference exists between blacks and whites, it's nothing compared to the universe that separates the blind from the sighted."

Laura made a quick instinctive gesture as if to ward off a ball flying at her. "I think we should end this conversation, Maxime."

That fellow is a Nazi, a blind Nazi. If you searched his mind you'd probably find a diabolical dream of a world dominated by unsighted people and . . . Enough, no need to go any further. What's eating him is jealousy, pure and simple. He wanted Laura himself and I have her—the rest is nothing but talk, malignant talk.

Maxime had stopped and we drank in silence.

And what if the bastard was right? Even before he began, I had felt excluded, an outsider, merely because I was the only one who could see. Maybe in time I would come to believe that Laura had eluded me, that I would never be able to understand her because she was so different. Then perhaps I would realize that she belonged to Maxime, that his world and hers were the same. She knows that he is young, rich, handsome . . . Good lord, how can I compete—me, a middle-aged teacher, poor, ordinary, liverish, near-sighted, and heaven knows what else. If I were to put Maxime on one side and myself on the other, the contrast would be so catastrophic that Laura would surely throw me out and fall into the arms of this superb male, this mixture of angel and demon.

"Will you have supper with us?"

My tone was scarcely convincing. Maxime stood up. "No, I'm expected elsewhere."

Stubbing out my cigarette, I offered to take him home.

"That's not necessary. There's a taxi station at the corner. I know my way perfectly. Besides, I have my scepter." He gripped his white cane. "With this thing, I'm monarch of the streets."

Walking ahead, Laura brushed lightly against him as she went to open the door.

My heart was beating fast. It's always at moments of farewell that important things are finally said. He knew I'd be listening, but that wouldn't stop him.

"See you soon, Laura. You're on the wrong path, you know. This man is your last link with the world of sight. You haven't broken off with it yet, although it has broken off with you; you haven't achieved full independence. When you do, you'll turn to me. And that will happen sooner than you think."

The door slammed. From the hall she turned and came toward me and I could see her lips trembling. She leaned against me, her forehead against my chest, her hair trailing between my fingers.

"He's mad. He has scared me ever since the first time I met him."

My voice was unsteady. "Maxime Dracula has gone to suck the blood of some solitary passer-by before returning to his crypt. Forget about him."

She nodded. I understand, Laura. It's not always easy to forget. Some of his words weigh heavily, so heavily it seems I can still hear them echo in the room.

"It's hot."

I opened the window and she joined me, leaning against the sill. Our elbows touched.

Through half-opened windows, television sets sent milky, bluish lights into the night. The sounds rushed toward us, a hubbub of cries, the muffled stamp of hooves galloping over dry hard sand.

"A wild Western," Laura said.

I nodded. It's strange to hear the fury and commotion of the old American West reverberate in the night air of Paris. The sky over our roof was so far from the breadth of an Arizona sky. A single star appeared between the bell towers of the Trinité, a small diamond sparkling in a smoke-rose jewel case, the colors of the moonless night.

In the Rue de Berne, empty at this hour, the roofs of cars parked along the sidewalks glistened softly as the sound of bugles heralded the oncoming cavalry and the closing scene of the Western.

We heard a loud sigh of relief. It was the daughter of our downstairs neighbor. The child must have been watching the flight of the last Apaches. In the covered wagon the survivors would be embracing as John Wayne pulled up his reins. Like Laura, I couldn't see the screen but the scenes unfolded beneath my eyelids and neither a horse nor a rifle shot escaped me.

"He's really a sick fellow," Laura murmured.

Damn it, she was still thinking about Maxime. What sort of evil seed had the man sown? Never mind, I'll prove too strong for him! I'll take Laura off and rid her of the fear that still haunts her. We'll plunge into the green waters of the sea and lean back to gaze at the golden haze of the cities suspended above us on the cliffs.

I grabbed her by the shoulders. "I, Jacques Bernier, by the grace of our Holy Father the Pope and in obedience to my gracious sovereign, offer you, Lady Laura, aid and assistance. For you I will conquer the omnipotent Prince of Darkness. I suggest that you on your mare and I on my palfrey get the hell out of here at the crack of of dawn."

Laura brushed my cheek with her lips. "Where do you want to go?"

"I haven't the faintest idea. We've just come from the south, in the east there are the battlefields of the Marne, and the west is jammed with tourists heading for camp sites in Brittany, in the north there's just coal and gaspits and . . ."

"Bruges!" She shook my hand as if we'd just made a deal. "Belgium. Bruges! I've always wanted to go there. There was a time when I did a good deal of traveling but I never managed to find a free weekend for Bruges. Shall we go?"

"Do they have beer?"

"Light beer."

"How about mussels?"

"Yes, with french fries."

"The sea?"

"A boundless sea."

"Flemings?"

"Hordes of them."

"Church chimes?"

"Lots."

"You're sure?"

"Positive."

"Okay, we'll go."

* * *

She's asleep. In the east, the rims of the metal roof-gutters are tinged with a dull light. Toward the Étoile the light is paler. The smoke from my Gauloise rises straight up in the air and shimmers in the chilly dawn. Piece by piece in the sky, like torn rags, the last shreds of night are disappearing. A thick cloud still hovers over there, toward the nineteenth *arrondissement*. There are corners of Paris where the day dawns more slowly.

In two hours we'll be far away.

# Amphitrite

*I* swear it's as flat as the palm of my hand. There isn't a soul around. Just run straight ahead."

She was dancing up and down on one foot and clinging to me. "Obviously, you'll beat me. I haven't run in four years."

"I haven't run in thirty, so neither of us is in top form. Go ahead, let's see who'll be first in the water. It's about a hundred yards from here."

"Is anyone in the water?"

"I told you, not a soul. They're all having lunch at this hour. Well, are we going or aren't we?"

"We're going."

"Get set. One, two, three, *go!*"

The sand was running through my toes, my knees were pumping up and down like pistons as my feet pounded the beach. Laura dashed ahead of me, her face tilted skyward, her heels raising drifts of sand. She was veering a little to the left but it didn't matter; the beach was deserted as far as the eye could see. We were the only two vertical objects in the immensity of the horizon.

She had a three-yard gain on me. I was panting, breathing in and out simultaneously, my respiration all muddled, my toes sticking more and more to the sand. She was going to win, damn her!

I spurted, legs working frantically, my heart about to explode. I gained a yard, then two, but I was puffing like a seal.

She heard me and groaned, then ran faster, as if her life depended on it. I didn't want to lose. I tackled her by the waist as she was in full flight and fell on her at the edge of the sea.

"You bastard, I was winning."

She was gasping for breath and we lay down on the beach, spent, our lungs aching.

The sand was wet and sticky. Laura wore a black bikini, very simple. After three tries I was finally able to emit a half-strangled sound.

"What did you say?"

I gulped more fresh air before answering: "I said you look very nice in that bathing suit, very chic and charming."

"Shall we go in?"

"That's what we came for."

It was all yellow and blue, the blue of the sea and the sky ahead of us, the yellow of the beach at our backs. We were at the water's edge.

Laura jumped up and down in the water. "It's pretty cold."

"That's because you're a sissy, I've already dived in."

"I don't believe a word of it."

We had to walk far out before the water reached our waists. She was heading straight into the sun, her arms crossed as if she wanted to step through it. It seemed as if the water would never get deeper, as if we could keep right on walking to the end of the world on this soft sand that slipped away under our feet with the ebb and flow of the waves.

Boxing at the empty air, Laura leapt up twice like a flying fish.

"Are you quite sure you're feeling all right?"

"Go to hell," she replied, then explained: "I've gotten so used to measuring my movements that now, when for once I'm sure I won't knock over a tea-set or poke my fingers in somebody's eye, I'm making the most of it. You'll just have to excuse me, old boy."

Splash! She went in. With her two hands cupped like a seashell, she threw water at me, her aim amazingly accurate.

It's hard to run in the water, but Laura thrashed ahead, then dove in and swam off. I went in more gradually and swam a careful breast stroke, keeping my head above water—I panic when my head goes under.

There she was on my left, swimming the crawl like a champion, cutting a furrow in the water.

"Where are you?"

"Over here."

Her fingers clutched me and I stood up. We still weren't over our heads. The water reached only to our chests—but we had gone a long way out. We were alone— the sky, the sea and us. Distorted by the water, our legs looked strange, like twisted branches, undulating gently.

"Kiss me, my love."

Salty, wet, warm lips—a sea-scented kiss, full of summer.

"Do you think we could make love in the water?"

"I don't see why not. But I think I should warn you that about a mile back there, on the land, I can see restaurant balconies jammed with diners carrying field glasses. As soon as they spot a couple in the water, they can't resist, they take a long hard look, because you never can tell . . ."

"Okay. It's too bad that all sighted people are voyeurs.

Shall we swim out a little farther? I'd like to go where it's over my head. Then we'll swim back."

Off we went. At first I had trouble keeping up with her, then she slowed down. After swimming quite a distance, we lay on our backs, resting. Out of the corner of my eye I could see her, floating gently like an anchored boat.

"I don't know where I am any more, I can only get my bearings vertically, the air above, the water beneath. Horizontally, I'm completely disoriented. But it doesn't matter because I know I won't bump into anything—only the sea can do this for me."

We had turned around and were swimming back, she going more slowly to prolong the pleasure, sometimes leaping then diving like a porpoise.

Once out of the water, the sharp wind gave me goose flesh. "Aren't you cold? Shall we run?"

"No, I'm dead tired."

I had forgotten our towels, so we lay down on the burning beach, our faces toward the sun. I covered her with the hot powdery sand and gradually she stopped shivering.

"I'd give ten years of my life for a cigarette."

There were some beach umbrellas behind us. Their faded red canvas swelled at times like sails and were swept by gusts of sand that gently fell away, rustling like dried grain.

The striped canvas flaps of two abandoned folding chairs fluttered weakly.

Her eyes were closed and her hand kept shaping and reshaping the same pile of sand. The sun blazed. On my left a family had just returned to the beach: umbrellas, folding chairs, shrimping nets, beach bags, thermos bottles. It was time to leave.

"Are there any gulls?"

"There's one floating right above you. It's almost

motionless. There! Now it's heading toward the sea . . .
I can't see it any more."

For a moment Laura seemed thoughtful. "How about
swimming again tomorrow?"

"Sure. We have to get back in shape."

She stood up. "Where are we going for lunch?"

"I've no idea. But I'll buy you the best mussels on the
North Sea. *Avanti!*"

She seemed to hesitate for a moment, as if suddenly
lost in all the space around her. Then she got up and
headed purposefully toward the sea.

"Wait for me, I'm going back in once more."

Alone now, Laura walked on and on. The waves broke
around her knees. Head raised, she stretched out her
arms.

A strange feeling came over me as I watched her ad-
vance in the water. For the first time I was seeing her
from a distance. At this moment, she was entirely alone
in the world. With the sun beating down on her, the
water enveloping her, she seemed to be evaporating into
thin air. And as she herself vanished, everything about
her disappeared too: her smile, her past, her way of
smoking, drinking, loving. All that was left was a figure
gradually merging with the sea. That was what she really
wanted, I could sense it: to be nothing but a body moving
in space, a microscopic being lost in the world's immensity, experiencing only this elemental pleasure.

Her hair, which for an instant floated on the water, was
no longer visible. I could see nothing but a faint frothy
furrow. I stood up, trying to follow it with my eyes.

She was very far out now, much farther than when we
had swum together. Although the waves were not high,
they hid her almost completely every now and then. She
had stopped swimming.

I walked down to the shore. I wanted to join her but
didn't dare. The instinct I'd had at the café near the

Casino when I refrained from lighting her cigarette took hold of me again. Laura wanted to be alone for the moment. To follow her would be a blunder.

Slowly she started back. A few more yards and she would no longer be over her head.

I stood at the edge of the water, my toes playing in the wet sand.

As she emerged, a spray of irridescent water glistened in her hair. Lowering her head, she shook it violently.

"Everything okay?"

At the sound of my voice she swerved lightly, holding out her wet hands.

"Fine."

The bath house smelled of wood and fresh paint. The sand stuck to my back, then trickled down, like tiny particles of shiny mica. I stuffed my socks in my pocket. A cracked mirror with a cigarette ad above it separated the rows of cabins. A quick look showed I had a terrific burn. For the rest of the trip I'd be walking around with a red nose. Everyone would take me for a lush. I'll have to tell Laura. Why cheat? Anyway, she would tumble to it as soon as my nose began to peel, a matter of a day or two. No point trying to hide it from her.

She was waiting for me at the refreshment bar, wearing a skirt I hadn't seen before. Her head bent to one side, she was brushing her hair. I watched the glinting grains of sand as they fell.

"I haven't seen that skirt!"

She twirled around like a mannequin at a fashion show. "You haven't seen anything yet. I've brought along a pair of Mexican pants that will cause a sensation."

We climbed the dunes, mounted the stairs and reached the sea wall. The windows of the houses reflected sea and sky as if there were nothing behind them, as if the houses were one large backdrop, like the stage set of a movie.

We entered a weathered brick tavern that smelled of

disinfectant and brine. A few minutes later we were stuffing ourselves like pigs. Once again I had forgotten my pills.

Nothing is heavier on the stomach than mussels. Especially the large number we ate. If you add the beer, the race on the beach, the swimming, it was enough to stagger a construction worker.

"I'd thought of driving to Bruges. In fact I was going to suggest a few educational trips to museums and that sort of thing. But how about a siesta instead?"

She patted her stomach cautiously. "You're having a terrible influence on me. I usually pick at my food but you're encouraging me to eat myself sick. Pretty soon I'll have rolls of fat like you. But those mussels were marvelous! I don't think I'll ever forget them."

"Are you in favor of a siesta?"

"You haven't noticed, but I've already begun mine."

The key was huge, like a jailkeeper's. The room faced a narrow courtyard. Along the walls a few anemic geraniums clung desperately to life. Opposite was a row of Flemish houses, graduating upward like steps. I pulled the curtains and lay down next to her.

Some sand still clung to her shoulders and her skin tasted of salt.

"Is that what you call a siesta?" she laughed.

"I must confess that in suggesting it, I had other ideas in mind."

"You don't say!"

"Yes."

Her hand came down and undid my belt buckle. "I'm deeply shocked," she murmured.

Beneath my eyes the sheet flickers as the sea swell carries us off in the growing storm. Laura, you are rocking back and forth with the ebb and flow of the tide . . . your hands and your lips move feverishly. The waves roll in, engulfing us—you welcome but fear them. They hollow out a deep whirlpool and, like a lost soul, you fling yourself into it, then call out to me. My love, my dearest buffeted love, let the waves dance, let the song of the seas swell and burst as if death, or life, were at the end of it.

And finally we reach the open sea; it yawns wide to pick us up and wash us against the shore, like spent and bewildered starfish.

Her hand slid down my neck and I could feel her heart gradually resuming its normal beat.

"Cigarette?"

It had become a rite, a ceremony she dubbed "the Gauloise for after." This was one of those moments when I've never known quite what to say, to her even less than to others. Besides, why words at all?

"Yes, a cigarette, please."

Her voice was still altered, as if a trace of passion lingered within each word. Side by side we smoked calmly, each balancing a precariously perched ashtray.

I couldn't get over it, I would never have believed I had such prowess: I've always had an idiotic fear of losing the power to make love, at least passably . . . I suppose many men of my age . . .

"What are you thinking of?"

"Nothing. I feel as if I'm floating on air. It's wonderful!"

Laura smiled. "I'm sure that's not true."

That girl has extra antennae. "What isn't true?"

"That you're thinking of nothing. I'm sure you're telling yourself this very minute that you're quite a guy, and you're as pleased as can be. Right?"

You have to be honest. "You're right. In the Middle Ages they would have called you a witch and burned you at the stake."

Placing her ash tray on the floor, she kissed me. "Would you get me a glass of water?"

I slipped on my shorts, went to the bathroom and let the cold water tap run. I filled the glass and took it to her, chortling all the while.

"What's so funny?"

"I put on my shorts before crossing the room. I've never been able to expose my rear end to a woman. This would make a funny story: a man so shy that he doesn't have the nerve to walk around naked in the presence of a blind woman."

She seemed partly amused, partly incredulous. "But why? Is there anything wrong with your rear end?"

"Not especially, I don't think. But it's a long time since I've had a glimpse of it, so I'm not the best judge. Anyhow, that's the way I've always been. I was even embrrassed when I took my army physicals."

At that she got such giggles that I had to pound her on the back to keep her from choking.

"You're crazy, you're absolutely cracked! You are positively the most repressed person I know. You ought to see a psychoanalyst."

"Not on your life. After he'd cured me, I'd probably walk up and down the corridors of the métro station completely nude under my open coat, to compensate for a lifetime of repression. I'd get myself arrested and hauled off to jail as a pervert or exhibitionist. Then I'd be struck from the list of teachers, dropped from social security, and forced to hold out my hat on church steps to people leaving after mass. Never! I'd rather remain just as I am."

Laura got up and planted herself at the foot of the bed, her hands on her hips. "I hope you've noticed that I don't have your problems."

I sighed. "Naturally. Your generation is more liberated than mine. By the way, is this the end of our siesta?"

"You promised me an afternoon of culture and I'm getting impatient."

We walked back to the car. The beach was jammed with bodies, some very pale, some burned. Children chased star-studded balls that the wind kept blowing away. A few sailboats were out and in the far distance loomed a large ship.

"It smells good," Laura said, breathing in the fresh salt air. "It smells of pirates."

Smoking Belgian cigarettes and nibbling on almond chocolate bars, we drove to Bruges, the radio turned high.

All the windows were down.

"On my right a wooden windmill, Flemish style."

"Is it turning?"

"No."

Twenty seconds of silence. "On my left, another windmill."

No answer. I let ten seconds elapse. "Still another, larger than the others."

"This is certainly a country of windmills," she said, nibbling on the chocolate.

"Yes," I answered, "and here's another, a very pretty one."

"Oh?"

Ten more seconds of silence. "Still on my right, another windmill, this one's made of stone."

Silence. No answer.

"And here's another, right ahead of it."

At the fifteenth windmill, Laura gently put her hand on my knee and said: "Jacques, will you do me a favor?"

"Certainly, my darling, what can I do?"

"Tell me exactly how many windmills you've seen since we left."

I laughed, then said: "None. Windmills are in Holland."

I whistled the tenor's aria from *Tosca*. "I really fooled you, didn't I?"

She sank down in her seat. "You idiot."

Bruges. We're coming to the first streets. The battle standards of the Burgundian kings fly above us in the square. Suddenly I am seized with panic. She'll never see all this loveliness, the splendor of the statues, the glint of the sun on the gold of the columns and balconies. She'll never see the palace reflected in the watered silk of the canals! What words can I use to describe this sumptuous dead city, forever frozen in its spectacular beauty? My God, I can't bear her to miss it!

We left the car just as the church bells began to sound a carillon. Pigeons wheeled above us and the heavy banners fluttered.

Her head tossed back, Laura smiled. It was then that I knew there was nothing to fear. Bruges would live in her memory, it was already part of her.

# Memling

*T*HE Memling museum.

She was describing a painting. "The portrait of a
woman. Her face is pale, like all Memling's faces, the
hair very dark and piled high on her head. A transparent
veil comes down to the mouth. You see the eyes and nose
through its fine mesh. She's wearing an embroidered
velvet bodice. She looks as if she has spent her life in a
chapel and her skin has taken on the color of the wax
tapers."

Scanning the paintings on the wall, I spotted it. "Here
it is, right here. Now you're standing directly in front of
it."

"Does it answer my description?"

"Exactly. You have a frightening memory."

The face was before us. The mouth seemed shaped for
the chanting of psalms and the eyes gazed at us tranquilly,
with perhaps a touch of disdain. Laura stood there for
quite a while, then we walked softly away, as you do in
museums.

We'd been here three days and the hours had passed
swiftly, punctuated by the sound of church bells, by the
carillons. We'd been drinking beer on café terraces over-

looking the gray canals, watching the boats glide by under the bridges.

We strolled the streets with their cobblestones and daydreamed in the parks where nuns and little old ladies in cotton stockings and dark shawls went by, heading for the cathedral at all hours of the day. Laura liked to saunter about the church aisles or sit in the center nave, listening to the organs or enjoying the silence.

We dined regularly in an Italian restaurant on the Rue de Liège, where the waitress soon got to know us and seemed fascinated by Laura. The first time we were there, Laura knocked over a salt cellar and the waitress realized immediately that Laura was blind. Since then she always brought us enormous helpings and showed us such shameless favoritism that we were amused.

I finally wrote to Anne. It felt as if a thousand years had elapsed since I had left her, and I was afraid I'd forgotten my own child. I asked to be remembered to everyone, hoped they were having good weather . . . Actually, I didn't know what to say: I'd never learned to put happiness in writing.

"Jacques."

"Yes."

She was dipping a piece of roll in her cup. It was ten o'clock and she hadn't finished breakfast. We'd felt lazy all morning.

"Will you do an errand for me?"

I complained, as I always do, as a matter of principle.

"It's not far, the stationery store where you bought the postcards last night, just across the street. Bring some drawing paper, an eraser, and a number two pencil."

If I hadn't been sitting I'd have fallen flat on my face. "What on earth for?"

"I'm going to draw you."

I looked at her. She didn't seem to be joking.

"You're not saying a word. Are you afraid I'll botch it?"

"No, that's not it, but all the same, I can't help thinking it will be difficult for you . . ."

"Yes, I know. You'll have to help me. Besides you forget that I studied for a year at the Beaux Arts before I got myself recycled into sociology. Not that I learned much, but anyway . . ."

I shaved quickly, bought what she asked for, even throwing in a pencil sharpener for good measure, and returned, conscious that this was no ordinary adventure.

She stationed me near the window, then sat down beside me. "Turn your head, I want your profile. There, like that."

Placing the index finger of her left hand on my forehead, she then drew it slowly down over the frame of my glasses, the bridge of my nose, my lips, chin and neck.

She was nervous. "There's only one way to do it and that's to make it life-size, I'll have to do it with a continuous stroke of the pencil, synchronizing my movements. I'll follow your profile with this finger of my left hand, and with my right hand I'll draw what I touch. The two actions have to be coordinated. Ready?"

"Ready."

I felt her hesitate. "How far is the pencil point from the paper?"

Without moving my head, I glanced at it out of the corner of my eye. "Less than half an inch."

"That's about right. Here I go."

Her finger slid slowly down my face as she drew. My nose, now my mouth . . . She began going off the paper, now she was entirely off. Should I tell her? She stopped. There wasn't room for the chin.

"Damn!"

Looking terribly upset, she quickly recovered, crumpled up the sheet of paper, and threw it away.

"The hardest part is to get the proportions right. I don't seem to be able to visualize the proper dimensions."

I thought about it. "You know what you need? A metronome."

She brightened. "You're not as dumb as you look. You'll have to say tick-tock, tick-tock, very regularly."

"Brilliant! Do I have to chime too? It will soon be eleven."

Unruffled, she placed the point of the pencil on a fresh sheet of paper.

"Now be ready. We'll start all over. Go ahead, say it regularly, like a clock."

"Tick-tock, tick-tock . . ."

She was doing better, finger and pencil were synchronized. We were finally at the jaw and neck line.

She heaved a long, loud sigh. "Let's see what it looks like."

The sharp pencil point had left only an imperceptible dent but enough to permit Laura to follow it with her finger. She ran over it several times, murmuring: "The curve of the chin is exaggerated. Where's the eraser?"

I handed it to her and watched as she went back into action. Totally absorbed in her work, she made a few changes, heaved another sigh, seized my head, gave me hell for moving it, drew her finger along the side pieces of my glasses, then followed the contour of my ear.

"You're tickling me."

"Don't be silly. I can't draw if I don't know what your ear looks like. Every ear is different. Do you know that the side pieces of your glasses are not horizontal?"

"That's the first I've heard of it."

"Well, I'm telling you. Your glasses are hooked over your ear above the level of your eyes. All right. There, I'm all through. You can go now. I don't need you any more."

A little miffed, I studied the sketch. She had just re-outlined my profile and was adding a few inside touches, using the indented pencil-tracing as a guide.

I stood up. "It would have been more exciting if you had sketched me in the nude. I could have bought a large fig leaf."

"Because of all your repressions, I thought you'd surely refuse to pose."

Somewhat at a loss, I wandered around the room. "Are you drawing me as you picture me or as I am?"

"The two are the same, there's really no difference. I'm the only woman who sees you as you truly are."

She eagerly returned to her drawing, working with both hands, the left guiding the right. It would take a long while: she could add further details only after rechecking the initial tracing each time.

"Shall I go or stay, talk or keep quiet?"

Suddenly she raised her head and addressed me sternly: "That's typical of people who live in close contact with the blind. Whenever a handicapped person is managing perfectly well on his own and no longer needs them, they don't know what to do with themselves, they're bored to death. Do whatever you please, go out, read your newspaper, look out of the window, do a crossword puzzle—whatever you want. All I ask is to be left alone."

"Don't be mad. I have the greatest respect for artists."

I lay down on the bed and glanced at the Belgian newspaper. It was unbelievable how little there was of interest in it. I'm always struck by this kind of thing when I'm abroad. Only in France, it seems, does anything ever happen.

Well, let's try the crossword puzzle. After ten minutes, I had filled in only one definition. An intellectual lot, the Belgians!

" 'Changes color with the seasons,' in eight letters. The first a C. Any ideas?"

Completely absorbed, she didn't bother to answer.

I tossed the paper to the floor, stretched out on the bed, and stared at the ceiling. A very fine ceiling, by the way.

It was curious how quiet this neighborhood was. Not a sound from the outside reached me; all I could hear was the scratch of pencil on paper. I yawned, turned this way and that a few times, looked at my watch: twelve-fifteen. Splashed with sun, Bruges seemed to be sleeping.

The way she bent over her drawing made it plain to me that she'd be working for a long time. There would be no stopping her until the job was completed.

I sent up a trial balloon. "Sorry to interrupt you, but I can see you'll be busy for quite a while. So I think I'll go down to the bookstore to buy something to read."

Plainly, I was just being a nuisance. She nodded her head but I doubt that she even heard me. I decided to be more precise.

"What do you think? Should I buy a collection of short stories or a work in several volumes?"

"*The Thibaults*," she cried, "buy the whole ten-book set of *The Thibaults* and also *Gone with the Wind*!"

I beat a hasty retreat. "Okay, okay. I think I'd better buy something to eat while I'm at it. Is there anything special you'd like?"

She had turned back to her drawing. "Yes, some sandwiches and beer. Also cigarettes. We don't have a single one left. I can't draw if I don't have a cigarette."

Half an hour later I was back with six bottles of Guinness, three huge sandwiches with eggs, tomatoes, ham, cheese and lettuce spilling out the edges, and four delicious-looking nougat pastries with buttered cream and meringue. I put everything on the bed and she handed me the drawing.

Turning it toward the light, I studied it intently. It was an extraordinary likeness.

The total effect on me was strange, to say the least.

So she really saw me! I looked the same to her as I do to others. She certainly hadn't flattered me. The elongated forehead was there, the slightly weak chin, and that line from nose to mouth that she often likes to follow with her patient, gentle fingers.

"How do you like it?"

"It's me, all right. Exactly! Can I keep it?"

"It's not finished. I still have to put in the shadings and make some small corrections. Then you can have it."

I kissed her, thrust a sandwich in one of her hands, a bottle in the other. We ate on the bed, sitting cross-legged and looking for all the world like a pair of those Indians you see in the cartoon strips.

Between bites of her sandwich, she said: "How about taking me shopping? If it would bore you, say so."

I had a mouthful of butter cream. "No. Why?"

"I want to send Edith a present. This is the first time in three years that we haven't spent our vacation together. I'm afraid she's a bit lonesome by herself. Anyhow, it would be a way of saying I'm sorry for leaving so suddenly."

"What sort of thing would Edith like?"

"A ring. She never wears any but adores having them."

We emptied five of the six bottles and ate all the sandwiches as well as the cakes. We went out as soon as Laura finished dressing. It was three o'clock.

# *Mickey Mouse*

$L$ OTS of people in the streets . . . Whenever we're in crowds, I've made it a practice to hold her very close, one arm around her shoulder, my body turned slightly toward her. As we make our way, passers-by brush against us. She walks briskly, chatting.

I'd noticed a street just off the main square with lots of shops. We certainly ought to find . . . There, that's the kind of place we're looking for.

It was a fashionable boutique, featuring Indian scarves, Afghan coats. Tibetan boots, Napalese necklaces—all probably manufactured nearby, on the outskirts of Liège or Namur.

I guided Laura to a counter where rings were heaped in a deep round container. She dug around, stirring them as if they were croutons in a soup bowl. "We'll have to look elsewhere. This is all junk," she said with finality.

We left. Flower vendors stationed themselves under the arcades as hordes of American tourists emerged from parked buses. Texans loaded down with cameras, little old ladies in flowered hats, chirping, clucking, jabbering, raising a cloud of face powder and filling the air with the

162

scent of powerful perfumes and deodorants. They swarmed all around us.

"You ought to warn me when we're entering a beauty parlor," Laura grumbled.

I dragged her away from the chattering flood in their gawdy prints but not before I recognized on one of them the same riotously colored dress that old Madame Rebolot had worn on graduation day. The other side of the street was less crowded, and we crossed at the traffic light.

A large department store at the corner resembled the Galeries Lafayette. No sooner had I remarked this than Laura, delighted, insisted on going there at once. When we entered, the place was so jammed that instinctively I drew back. Sensing my hesitation, she squeezed my arm.

"Are you afraid of all these people? Don't worry, I'll be your guide."

We took the escalator. "I'm going to buy you something, too. What would you like?"

She was happy and very excited. Never have I held the arm of a woman as full of life as Laura was on that particular afternoon. From every pore she exuded vitality, her laugh rang out, she was absolutely radiant in that big department store.

"I haven't any idea. You've taken me by surprise."

I was steering her between the counters. The jewelry section was at the other end of the huge floor.

"You must need a lot of things. I bet an old fuddy-duddy bachelor like you has bedroom slippers with pom-poms on them, Right?"

"Naturally. And in the winter I wear a long quilted nightshirt and a matching nightcap with a tassel. On really cold nights I even keep on my flannel underwear and wool socks when I go to bed."

Delighted, she kept nudging me with her elbow. "Oh,

I can just see you, with a cup of hot camomile tea on your bedside table."

"Of course. Right next to the drops for my heart and the glass for my false teeth. And I always keep cough drops under the pillow. I go to sleep sucking one, my feet on a hot water bottle under the comforter."

"Don't you burn your socks on the hot water bottle?"

I had no time to answer for we'd come to the jewelry counter. The saleswoman had the air of a wild rabbit, which was accentuated by a faint mustache. "What can I do for you?"

"I would like a ring, something without stones or pearls, a heavy geometric kind of ring in stainless steel or some such metal, if you know what I mean. Please let me feel each one. I can't see."

The wild rabbit turned red, scooped up some jewelry cases, and searched among them with frantic good will.

Why had she blushed when Laura told her she was blind? One of the mysteries of the human mind. She deposited her selection in Laura's palm.

"If these won't do, I have others." She watched as Laura's fingers flew over the rings.

"Not bad, this one. What do you think?"

It was a contraption of two steel cubes that fitted together unevenly, big enough to cover the entire knuckle. Laura put it on and seemed to like the sleek metal surface.

"Does it shine?"

"No, it has a dull finish."

She sighed, stroked an intricately looped affair that seemed to attract her, then set it aside and fingered the first ring again.

"I'll take this one, I like it better."

"Which would you have preferred for yourself?"

"The same one. I always buy Edith what I'd like for myself."

I turned to the wild rabbit, whose nose hadn't stopped twitching. "I'll take two of these."

Laura moved close to me. "I'm very touched. Is the other one for me?"

"You're an absolute genius! You guessed right the first time. Your thigh against mine is most disconcerting."

The wild rabbit heard me and her jaw fell. "Would you like me to gift-wrap two separate packages?"

"Yes," said Laura, "that would be nice."

The saleswoman left. Laura raised her mouth to mine and languorously bit my lower lip, taking her time. These blind people seem to think they can get away with anything.

"I shouldn't have let you do this. You won't have anything left of your teacher's pittance with a gold digger like me."

I pressed my index finger against the tip of her nose. "Don't worry. I've managed to put aside quite a nest egg. It's hidden under my mattress. I was going to buy a little thatched cottage for my golden years. Well, never mind! I'll just end up in an old people's home."

The saleswoman returned with the two packages wrapped in red and green paper with corkscrew ribbons.

"Over here, if you please."

We paid the cashier and Laura took my arm. "Now it's my turn to buy you a present. I'm going to select something useful. Take me to the men's department."

Her tone was so commanding I had no choice. But as we threaded our way between the counters, I timidly spoke up.

"You know, I really have everything I need: a coat for winter, a raincoat for spring and fall, a suit for everyday . . ."

Laura interrupted me with a gesture. "I'm not interested in what you have to say, I don't want your opinion."

Defeated, I followed.

She then embarked on a swift tactile ballet, touching shirts, feeling sweaters, stroking wools, corduroys, cottons, synthetics, circling around the counters. Every now and then I tried to register a protest, but she paid no attention.

"What you need most of all," she decreed, "is a turtleneck sweater, not too heavy, but warm enough."

"For heaven's sake, this is July!"

"But the nights are cool here. Anyway, you shivered the other evening in Ostende. As soon as there's the slightest breeze, your teeth begin to chatter. Did you think I didn't notice?"

"Okay, I'll admit it. But I've got my jacket."

"That's just it. I'm sick and tired of that jacket! You'll be much more comfortable in a sweater and at least you'll look athletic."

That was hitting below the belt. "But I'm not athletic and don't pretend to be. You saw for yourself the other day on the beach. Besides, I'm not the type to walk around in a turtleneck!"

She didn't listen, her fingers were stroking a particular sweater. With two fingers she followed the seam on the shoulders, then flung it against my chest.

"This should fit. You'll have to try it on."

Suddenly foreseeing all the agonies of the dressing room, I tried to talk her out of it. "Oh, not this one, it's absolutely hideous! Yellowish green and blue stripes, it's horrible."

She was grumbling at me when, in the nick of time, a saleswoman appeared. Not at all like a wild rabbit, she was more the type you would see at the show in the Crazy Horse Saloon, a stripper with a few too many pounds.

"May I help you?"

Very sweetly, and with a slow Machiavellian smile, Laura purred: "Forgive me, Mademoiselle, but I'd like some information: what is the color of the sweater I'm holding?"

The saleswoman didn't seem a bit surprised. She was evidently used to all kinds of silly questions. Very matter-of-factly, she replied: "It's written on the label, Madame, it's gray."

Silence. I coughed discreetly.

"Gray," Laura said.

"Yes," said the saleswoman, "gray."

"Are you sure it doesn't have green, blue, yellow, or red stripes?"

"No, Madame, this model only comes in solid colors."

"Thank you, Mademoiselle."

Laura turned to me. "You think you're so smart, don't you?"

I dug into the pile and brought out a brown one. "This is brown. I like the color better."

And there I was again in a dressing room! As always, the curtains didn't close, leaving the usual gap. I removed my shirt, tried on the sweater and looked at myself. Not bad at all. The collar hid my neck, which is a little too thin, the wool clung to my powerful torso. I came out, stomach pulled in, chest thrust forward, and Laura felt me, pulling on the wool. Very maternally, she inquired: "Does it seem tight under the arms? It's not uncomfortable?"

"No, it's perfect."

I was delighted. Of course, with something like this on, I'll have to stand up straight all the time. Some of my students wear turtlenecks, but I never thought the day would come when I'd be sporting one.

Laura and the saleswoman were engaged in a highly technical conversation about the best way to wash sweaters —cold water versus lukewarm, and so on, involving words like "drip-dry," "non-matting," "shrink-resistant."

"We'll take it," Laura said. "And now to the shirt department."

I protested. "But I've got plenty of shirts! There are at least two more in my suitcase."

"No!" Laura said, "I've had enough of those white shirts. They make me feel as if you've just come back from a wedding and forgotten your tie. I want something brighter for you. Give me your hand and take me to the shirt department."

Once there, I had to stick out my neck so that a third saleslady, this one the athletic type with damp hands, could measure it. She also unrolled her tape measure for my shoulders and my sleeve length. The Belgians really take their work to heart.

Laura chose three shirts: one maroon (I held out for at least one dark color) and two with bold stripes. One had canary yellow stripes on a mustard background. I could picture myself wearing it to school: the kids would have a great time selling tickets for a good look at the spectacle. Laura had the saleswoman describe the colors in detail. Then she bought them all.

As we passed the T-shirt counter, I said: "You know what I'd like best of all? A T-shirt with the words 'I love Mickey Mouse' across the front. If you'll also buy me a yo-yo, we can go and play in the park."

Her fingers squeezed mine very hard. "Are we in the T-shirt section?"

For a minute I panicked. I thought she was really going to buy one. I could see myself sauntering around Bruges with Donald Duck or Angela Davis stenciled across my chest. Actually, she did buy a T-shirt, but fortunately it was for herself. She kept it on, a black and green affair that fit her like a glove and made her look very young. When she walked over to me with the smile of an eighteen-year-old, I felt as though I were twenty and we were alone, meeting like young lovers at the edge of a Flemish canal—one of those straight quiet canals that flow toward the sea between banks of thistles and sad-looking trees.

That's how she was, Laura. Maybe it was because she could no longer see, that she was able to abstract herself from the crowd. All I know is that the minute she smiled at me, everything around us vanished—all the clamor, all the sound. The store too disappeared and there she was, waiting for me near the canal, a flower in her hand, one of those pale, late-blooming roses of autumn.

"Is it becoming?"

I came back to earth. "You look like Ursula Andress, but better."

Satisfied, she took my arm. "Come on, there are a few more things I want."

Rushing along, I thought we were going to buy up the store. On a real shopping spree, we dashed up and down, stopping at every floor like a couple possessed. Finally I came to my senses and called a halt.

"I'm dying of thirst. If I don't get a drink in three minutes, I'll drop in my tracks."

Our arms loaded down, we left and finally collapsed with our packages in an elegant tearoom near the Flanders bridge.

Through the stained-glass windows you could glimpse the tops of the palaces on the opposite bank. I downed my beer in a single gulp and examined our pile of purchases. There were records, a china tobacco jar for Simon, a large scarf for a friend of Laura's whom I didn't know, a suede jacket for Laura—apparently quite a bargain—some panty hose, my turtleneck, my shirts, and socks—ten pairs.

"Why ten?" I had asked.

"Because they take no room at all in your suitcase and it's more practical than washing your only pair every night in the hotel washbasin."

I tried to tell her that I had three pairs, that this was how I've operated for at least twenty years, but I was wasting my breath. I now had ten pairs of new socks. Farewell, my beloved nightly washing. My life was being turned upside down by this woman.

She was drinking. Her eyes shone above the white foam of the beer and she wiped her lips with the back of her hand like an ill-mannered child.

"We had fun, didn't we?"

"Yes, Laura, yes."

We'd certainly had fun.

# Carlos Monzon

TOMORROW the weather would probably turn ugly. Above the sea, the evening sky was filled with somber clouds. The streets were empty and the canal reflected only the darkening horizon.

We were in a dismal café. A solitary soldier was eating sausage and french fries in one corner; in another, a couple of tired-looking lovers were mechanically stroking each other's hair. Leaning against the wall, the waiter watched them, probably hoping that things would pick up for them and his day would end on a spicier note. Nearby, two tables from us, a chap in a tweed jacket was staring fixedly at his reflection in the mirror.

Laura put the tip of her match to a stub in the ashtray and with a surgeon's precision tore the cigarette paper to snuff out the smoldering tobacco.

She yawned and I yawned.

It was one of those moments—one among many—when life seemed to have reached a standstill, pulled up to rest like a winded racer. Everything was quiet and melancholy, our conversations died, nothing was happening, nothing seemed about to happen. For the present, limp and weary, we remained on the sidelines. All we could do was to wait for life to start up again.

That's the difference between life and the movies: films leave out the intervals when time hangs heavy. They string together only the most exciting episodes. Life, on the other hand, liberally deals out idle, bleak moments— even to those who live most intensely.

"How about going home?"

"If you'd like."

She too was making no effort, evidently feeling as I did that it would have been useless. In a small voice, she added: "This is a sinister joint. I'm sure the cellar is full of dead bodies."

We had ventured rather far from the center of the city and had walked quite a while before finding this unfortunate corner café. For some reason, all the cafés in Belgium seem to be located on corners.

We left. Laura kept stroking my sweater. "You're nice and warm in it, aren't you, young fellow?"

It was true, I couldn't resist wearing it constantly.

I gazed up at the sky.

"Do you really want to go to the beach tomorrow? The weather looks very uncertain and I bet it's going to pour."

"Let it. I love the ocean in the rain. It's even more beautiful then."

A breeze as chilling as a November wind greeted us along the quays. The first street lamps were just ahead.

"Good lord," Laura said, shivering. "What a country! I should have worn my jacket."

A billboard for a movie was tacked to a wall but the light was so dim I let go her hand for a second to get close enough to read it. She kept right on walking.

What were they showing? *Once Upon a Time in the West.* Damn! I had seen it. Maybe we'd go to the Memling Theater where they had an American thriller with Rod Steiger.

Then I heard a shout.

There were three people under the arching street lamp: a man, Laura, looking petrified, and a small boy on the ground.

The man leaned down. Then, without bothering to find out if the child had been hurt, he looked up and yelled: "Can't you see where you're going?"

I hurried toward them in time to hear Laura say, very simply, "No, I can't."

I knew she wouldn't say she was blind, that was out of the question. I hoped the man would realize it even though he was furious.

He saw me and scooped up the child with one arm. A rough, burly fellow with a face as round as an Edam cheese and a Hitler-type mustache. Not realizing we were together, he winked at me, then turned to Laura.

"You can streetwalk along the canal, but next time watch where the hell you're going."

I should have stopped myself but I couldn't. Before I had time to think, I blurted it out: "She's blind, you dirty bastard!"

Either I had shouted too loud or he was unwilling to understand. He just fastened on the insult.

"What did you call me? Say it again." Cupping his hand to his ear as if he were hard of hearing, he leaned forward, a stupid, crafty expression on his face. He had a good forty pounds' advantage over me and obviously knew it. In the most infuriating way, he kept repeating: "What did you call me? I'm not sure I got it."

Fear flooded through me from head to guts. I felt a wild urge to take to my heels. Instead, raising my voice, I repeated: "You dirty bastard."

I saw the blow coming and took it on the shoulder. Laura flung herself against me but didn't block a beautiful opening for a jab at the guy's face. My fist shot out and I thought I'd smashed every knuckle. Hitler fell back a good yard as blood cascaded from his nose. Instinctively, he leaned forward to avoid splattering his tie.

"Get the police, Marcel, I'm bleeding."

Laura lunged toward the voice, her fingers clenching my wrist so hard it hurt. I was trembling like a leaf.

"You idiot, I told you, I'm blind, *blind!* Do you think I knocked your kid down on purpose?"

He was breathing hard but his mind worked so slowly you could almost see the ideas laboring around in his thick skull.

Finally he said: "I'm bleeding. He's going to pay for this."

Then he started to come toward me. Some people were coming out of a café across the street and others were passing by us. That gave me a few seconds to think.

I stepped back with Laura still clinging to me. I could feel the wall against my back. At this point I decided I'd had enough—there were now forty years of timidity to get rid of! And I couldn't bear the thought that Laura might guess how scared I was. I would have to stand up to that obstinate imbecile who was now coming toward me like a bulldozer.

I shook Laura off and met him head-on. I must have landed one again because I heard him groan. Then suddenly everything went black.

I felt the ground fly up to meet me. My cheek touched gravel. There was a loud rush, I came to, the lights seemed too bright, I saw legs, trousers, and heard people talking Flemish. I stumbled up. Laura was speaking to two men but I couldn't see them clearly. With bits of enamel grating between my teeth, I walked over to her and we left, moving quickly. I was aware that everyone was staring after us. Another group had gathered across the street and stood there, following us with their eyes.

The light in the room was dazzling. I sat down, my legs

like cotton, my hands still trembling a little. The left side of my jaw hurt the most, the pain shooting up from ear to temple. Laura was gently pressing a washcloth against my cheek.

I watched the water drip over my sweater and onto the bedspread.

"Why did you have to call him a dirty bastard?" she said gently.

I had a pain in my shoulder too; it throbbed all the way to my neck. I guess Roland must have been in the same sorry state after the battle at Roncevalles.

"Because it seemed to me an accurate statement."

She didn't answer. She had pulled back my lip and was pressing on my teeth.

"Isn't one a little loose?"

She looked so worried it made me laugh.

"I lost a crown, but otherwise they're okay. You should have warned me that he had a sledgehammer up his sleeve."

Her fingers were feeling my jaw. "You're so lucky your glasses didn't break. Lie down, it will be easier. I'll keep giving you hot compresses. Otherwise, by tomorrow you'll be black and blue all over."

I stretched out on the bed while she went into the bathroom. I've seen this in quite a few movies: the handsome hero, a nice guy and a real scrapper, luxuriates as he lets a gorgeous dame treat his wounds. Well, this time I'm the hero!

Yes, but usually the hero comes out on top, whereas tonight. . . . Yet he was the one who got the hell out of there, that bastard; besides, I landed a real haymaker, a beauty, something to remember.

"Laura."

"Yes."

"It's too bad you couldn't see what I did to him. I

landed a real haymaker. It's a punch Carlos Monzon is always trying to land, but he doesn't connect most of the time."

"Who is Carlos Monzon?"

"A boxer. A world champion."

She came back with another hot washcloth and a towel. "Take off your sweater."

I complied, giving her a blow-by-blow account of the fight. I've often watched matches on television, not that I'm so crazy about them, but I watch them anyway.

"He came toward me like a mountain of muscle. Very scientifically, I waited for an opening. When he lowered his guard, wham! I let him have it! A tremendous haymaker! If a referee had been on the job, he'd have stopped the match then and there. And the second time, thanks to my footwork . . ."

"Lie still and hold on to the towel."

The hot washcloth against my cheek seemed to be drawing off the pain. It felt good.

". . . thanks to my footwork, I managed to land a jab. But then I slowed down for a split second. He took advantage of this to connect. The fact that it was dark also helped him. Otherwise . . . What on earth are you doing?"

She had put the rolled-up towel under my chin, pulling the two ends tight and tying them on top of my head. "There, that will hold, you look like a beautiful Easter egg."

I got up and looked at myself in the mirror above the washstand. My God, what a sight! Never in all my life had I seen anything more ridiculous. Another ludicrous touch: a corner of my mouth was swollen.

Laura giggled. Some tension still lingered but she was beginning to relax.

"How about a cigarette? It's customary to have one

after a fight—it's always done."

She lit one and gave it to me. "Say, I thought you were the quiet, nonviolent type. What got into you?"

I snorted. "You must be kidding. I'm a born fighter. It was lucky for him that he ran away—I would have made mincemeat out of him."

Rubbing her thigh, she made a face. "I'm afraid I hurt that kid. He must have been running when I bumped into him. As it was, I almost fell over him. In a way, the fellow was right to bawl me out. If you can't see, you shouldn't be strolling about alone."

"You weren't alone. I was only a few feet from you and there was nothing in the way, not a single obstacle. It was just rotten luck, that's all. Anyway, you've a perfect right to walk about, you're not a public menace."

"But I am! You saw for yourself. And besides, I was frightened. I suddenly felt surrounded by danger—unexpected movements, collisions . . . When I first became blind I often had nightmares about walking on a road with cars speeding by, I could feel the currents of air as they passed. I'd see powerful headlights, hear the screech of tires, horns honking . . . That man, his voice, brought it all back to me."

She began to tremble, then grew tense trying to hide her nervousness. She pushed my hand away from her arm. "You can see for yourself, you can't depend on a blind woman—one incident and she cracks up."

I didn't know what to do or say, she seemed suddenly so vulnerable, so utterly defenseless. For the first time I saw her as a cripple, infinitely fragile, exposed to every hazard. To Laura, the edge of a sidewalk, the corner of a table, a chair, a stairway, a cat—anything at all—could prove fatal. For a few seconds only, just time enough to look at a billboard, I wasn't there to protect her. And she, acting instinctively, had gone on walking a few steps alone . . . That had been enough to make her realize her true condition.

"It was my fault. I shouldn't have left you alone on the sidewalk."

She cried out violently: "Why shouldn't you look at a billboard for a few seconds! You've got every right to, you're not chained to me! No, it wasn't your fault at all."

I raised my voice. "I see no reason to quarrel. We happened to run into an idiotic bastard who was just spoiling for a fight. That kind of thing can happen to anyone."

She laughed but her eyes were filled with tears. I held her very tight. For quite a while she sobbed and sobbed. What a great pair we were—she miserable, her face dripping with tears that washed away her make-up, and me with a towel tied around my head and a swollen lip.

We held each other close for a long time, then I got a washcloth and wiped away her tears.

"Save it," she said, "we've used up all the washcloths tonight."

I sensed that it was over, that the crisis had passed. I clowned around the room, simulating the noises of a boxing match, giving the shouts of the crowd, the sounds of punches landing, the gong, the advice of the trainer. Then suddenly there was a bang on the wall. It came from next door. The guests didn't seem pleased at one-thirty in the morning to be treated to a rerun of a middleweight fight in Madison Square Garden.

Laura had completely calmed down. "They're probably not sports fans," she whispered. "We'd better go to sleep."

After I refused one more compress, we finally got to bed. I felt exhausted but tranquil, relaxed. The incident was over.

She kissed me on the forehead like a mother kissing a child who had just undergone an operation.

"Good night, Laura Bérien."
"Good night, Carlos Monzon."
I was already asleep.

# Niagara

*I* shut off the windshield wipers. Large drops immediately swept the windshield and the rain drummed down on the roof.

She was pulling at the zipper of her slicker. It caught, she tugged, finally it closed. Swathed in the shiny yellow oilskins, she looked like a sailor about to board a trawler.

"Do you want to go anyway?"

"Of course! A few drops shouldn't scare us off."

"A few drops" was quite an understatement. The rain streamed down the windows of the Casino. In front of us the beach resembled a large khaki blanket that was gradually getting soaked. Not a soul around, naturally.

We got out of the car. Her hair glistened with water and she lifted her face to the sky, closing her eyes. The drops, in tiny liquid explosions, pelted her forehead and lips.

The sea, drowned in the fog, was invisible.

"I can feel the mist."

We stepped over the rivulets that had formed in the sand. She wore boots, but my feet, protected only by oxfords, were bound to get soaked. And I had planned to wear those shoes for at least another year! They'd be ruined. I'd have to treat myself to a new pair.

"How about walking out to the sea wall?"

"If you want."

Above us, the heavy swollen clouds formed distended curtains that might presently split open to pour tons of water down on us like cataracts. For the moment, at any rate, the rain had subsided, but we were moving ahead into a deep cotton-wool fog.

"You can't even see the beacon. It's all white out there."

I turned around. Behind us the coast had disappeared in the dense mists. We were isolated, cut off from the world, surrounded by impenetrable cotton. Pushed by the wind, the fog was rolling in from the sea and all around us the haze was growing thicker.

"We're lost, Laura. You can't see three feet ahead—only a little bit of the sea wall, that's all."

She smiled. "I've always loved to walk in this kind of weather. Is it white all around us?"

"Yes, white and gray."

I cocked an ear. I couldn't tell if it was the constant pounding of the ocean waves or a more distant rumbling, but beyond the fog, something immense and dangerous seemed to be moving toward us.

"Right near the beacon," Laura said, "there's that stairway that leads down to the beach. Let's take it."

"I'll have to find it first."

I couldn't even distinguish the outlines of the beacon. With my hands I guided myself along the cold stone wall as the rain quickened. My raincoat was already saturated and I might as well have removed my glasses. I couldn't see a thing.

Here were the iron steps, rusty and slippery. The sand below was full of small red puddles as if the rain had stripped the steps of color.

We descended to the beach. Laura was breathing

heavily and wiping away the water that ran down her cheeks. I knew why she loved this place. It was bare, empty, devoid of obstacles, spelling freedom for her.

Then suddenly, without any warning, the storm erupted, and, as if all the floodgates had been opened, a thousand Niagaras fell on us.

She shouted something in my ear but I couldn't hear a word. It was a vertical high-pressure torrent, impossible to take shelter anywhere. Laura was cut off from me, isolated by sheets of falling water. We ran, but there was no point in running, the rain was pouring down my back in a glacial stream and the flooded sand had taken on the color of old mustard.

"It's the end of the world!" I shouted.

She ran ahead, hands in pockets, the sand clinging to her boots. I followed as fast as I could, telling myself it would be the limit if we lost each other.

"Laura, wait for me."

She stopped and turned toward me, raindrops suspended from her eyelashes. No sooner had I joined her than everything suddenly stopped. The rain had ceased as abruptly as it had begun, the floodgates were closed. Her fingers felt my hair.

"Poor little wet doggie . . ."

I began to shiver. We would certainly get the grippe after such a drenching. In desperation, I made a stab at getting her home: "We ought to go back, darling. We're soaked; we'll catch our death of cold."

She frowned. "That's a typical old-bachelor remark. You're longing for your camomile tea and your hot water bottle."

I was miffed. "I suggested it for your sake, to keep you from catching cold. Personally, I like nothing better than getting completely drenched."

She pouted scornfully. "You say that to show off, but you hate it. You're just an old city boy, you never go out

without your umbrella, you avoid the quays along the
Seine so the dampness won't give you rheumatism. Did it
ever occur to you that it's pleasant to walk in the rain,
that it falls on you directly from the heavens without
any intermediary, like a gift?"

"Of course, I love it, I adore it. I just wanted to be
careful."

An explosion of laughter. "I'll say you're careful! I can
tell by your voice that you're dying to go back to the
hotel to drink a hot grog. Admit it, at least."

She was really beginning to get under my skin. I would
have to speak up loud and clear if I were ever to be left
in peace.

Successive veils of clouds were lifting, like curtains
at the theater. The sea reappeared, still hazy, shimmering
and indistinct like a phantom. The city was emerging from
the mist, gray on aluminum gray.

"I love the water, probably more than you. Come to
think of it, I'm going in for a swim."

That dumfounded her all right.

"But you didn't bring your swimming trunks."

"Given the state I'm in, it doesn't really matter.

I pulled her toward the water. She resisted, then gave
in. We splashed through the puddles in the sand. There
we were; we had reached the water's edge. I took off my
shoes, jacket and raincoat and handed them to her.

Keep these for me." No point in removing my socks,
they couldn't get any wetter. "See you later."

I just left her there, holding my clothes, and went in.
As always after a heavy rain, the water was warm. It
made my trousers cling to my legs and the effect was
curious but not at all unpleasant.

Here I was swimming, and it was marvelous, as tepid
as a bath. When I floated, air pockets formed between my
skin and my shirt, giving a fine balloon effect. I felt in
top form. Way over there, hardly visible on the shore,

Laura waited, a tiny lost silhouette. Certain that she was filled with admiration, I felt very smug. Who could have foreseen, when I left Paris for the Mediterranean, that I would be swimming in the North Sea? And with my clothes on too. Life is full of surprises: I had almost forgotten that.

Let's not push a good thing too far, though. A few more strokes and I'll go back.

I came loping toward her. Unruffled, she was strolling up and down.

"Hello!" I squeezed the water out of the dripping trousers. "Wonderful dip," I commented. "I hope you were impressed. Would you hand me a cigarette?"

"In the pocket of your trousers."

Damn! She was right. I reached in and extracted a mess of spongy tobacco and wet paper.

"All the same," Laura said softly, "there are times when I'd give a lot to be able to see you. Try to describe the look on your face this very minute."

"I'm smiling," I replied. "Good humor, intelligence, and kindness are written all over my face. Couldn't you have reminded me before I went in that the cigarettes were in my pocket?"

"A man as smart as you should think of everything."

I wanted to answer but sneezed instead. We returned to the car.

"Now," Laura said, "how about buying me a drink in Ostende?"

I sneezed again. "Don't be cruel. I'm catching pneumonia right now. Let's go back to the hotel."

She felt my clothes. "You can't drive like that. It will take us at least a half hour to get back and you'll be shivering. There's a sweater in the trunk."

I took off my shirt and put on the sweater. Then we got into a terrible hassle about my trousers. In the end she won out. Squirming, twisting, taking all sorts of covert precautions and bumping my knee on the steering wheel, I finally managed to remove my trousers and wrap myself in the car rug.

"Don't be so timorous. There's not a soul in the parking lot."

I jumped at that. "There's one thing I'd like to know: how in heaven's name can you tell? Are you blind or aren't you?"

"I am. And you're the king of idiots."

"Well, we make a fine couple."

I kissed her. She offered me a cigarette. She had put a package in her slicker.

We started off. Truth compels me to admit that after a mile or so, thanks to my dry sweater, warm rug, heater turned on, and cigarettes, I was feeling fine. In fact, a gentle warmth began creeping over me and I felt absolutely euphoric.

Laura put her hand on my neck. "Are you all right?"

"Just fine. Thanks to you, I won't have to go to the hospital. From not on I'll always take your advice. I never thought it would be so pleasant to wear a skirt. This is the first time I've tried it and it's sensational."

We passed two villages and some low farmhouses. In the rearview mirror I could see the sky. The clouds were still thick and solidly massed over the sea.

We came to a crossroad and it was shortly after that that I felt the steering wheel stiffen. Suddenly the car seemed to become heavier, as if it were hauling a truckload of horses. I braked, blinked my turning signals and stopped the car on the side of the road. I had guessed the trouble—there could be no doubt about it.

"What's the matter?" Laura asked.

"A flat."

"A flat?"

"Yes, I've got a flat tire."

Never in my life have I heard a woman laugh so hard. She had to repeat herself three times before I managed to make out what she was saying.

"You'll have . . . you'll have to get out and change it."

The thought of having to put on my soaking trousers gave me goose flesh.

"Forget about your trousers," Laura hiccupped. "Just keep your skirt on. Some gallant driver will give you a hand."

There were quite a few cars on the road. I had to repeat all the squirming and contortions in reverse order.

"I'd be delighted to help you," Laura said, "but you know we blind people aren't much use."

I finally got out, shivering in my icy trousers, and began to get the tools together—the contraption for removing the lugs, the jack, and the rest. Then I went to work. Laura stood under a tree; to make everything just perfect, it had begun to rain again. This was my second drenching of the day and my spirits had reached a new low.

I began to revive after a second hot grog in the back room of a Bruges café. I was wearing two sweaters, one over the other, and a dry pair of trousers. My only complaint was that they hadn't lit the stove.

Laura took my hand. "The king of idiots is nice and warm now, isn't he?"

I growled. Suddenly she said: "What about heading in another direction?"

I swallowed a mouthful of burning rum. "Sure, if you'd like. But for God's sake, let's not go north! After today, I'd like a warmer climate."

She seemed to hesitate. "How about first returning to Paris? We could decide there."

I liked the idea. In fact, I liked all our comings and goings: Menton-Paris, Paris-Bruges, Bruges-Paris, Paris

—well, we'll see. That's what it means to be free, after all, to come and go as you please, aimlessly . . .

"Okay! We'll head for Paris."

We treated ourselves to a third hot grog.

# Tatania

THE queen buried her face in her hands, and her heavy brocaded skirt, swirling in a circular movement, swept over the stairs to the throne. Rooted to the spot, she contemplated the guards, their sharp pointed halberds catching the light of the torches.

Trumpets blared, the prince appeared. A few rapid strides and he seized the heavily bejeweled hands of the queen.

Her metallic voice rose, stressing the final syllables: "I was not aware that you had come."

She drew herself up and her scarlet fingernails seemed to tear at the watered silk of her bodice. "What a mistake you have perpetrated, nay, what a lie, Gregor! An order signed by your hand has forced me to remain in this sinister place and to appear before you."

Sighing, Laura murmured: "I'm bored stiff!"

I leaned toward her and whispered: "Do you want to leave?"

"*Shhh!*"

We kept quiet. The fellow behind us looked most disagreeable. Obviously he didn't want to miss a single word. He'd probably bought season tickets.

On the stage the discussion continued. The queen seemed to be in a temper. "If the people hear of your plans, beware! Out of respect for their late king they will make you pay dearly for your villainy."

His hand toying with the scabbard of his sword, Gregor took heed. "You are right, my queen," he roared. "There is no time left for subterfuge. Guards, sieze the lady!"

The queen extended a taut arm to her tormentor. "God will judge you, Gregor. When the hour of your death tolls, it will herald an eternity of suffering!"

Curtain.

A light patter of applause as faint as a spring shower. There were about fifteen in all in the entire theater.

Two more acts to come. I didn't think we could stick it out to the end. As we made our melancholy way to the bar, the handful of spectators glanced at one another suspiciously, each apparently wondering how the other could have had the ridiculous idea of coming to this place.

I looked around. "Paneled ceilings, crystal chandeliers with tear drops, plush-covered sofas, tapestries, it's dowdy, dingy, and empty."

"Let's go to the window."

We crossed the foyer. Behind the bar a blonde with masses of curls was disconsolately awaiting the end of the intermission. Her lone customer was staring resignedly at his glass of Coca-Cola.

Laura pressed her forehead against the pane. As she turned, lights danced in the pupils of her eyes. "What do you see?"

"Not much, some roofs, chimneys, over there a cupola. Far in the background, the towers of Montparnasse."

"I always liked to look out of windows in a theater," Laura said. "When I was a child I once saw a movie where a woman dreamily leaned on the balcony of a window and behind her, brilliantly illuminated, you could see the crowd with officers laced up in their frogged uniforms. It was snowing, and I wondered why she didn't catch cold, her shoulders were completely bare. One of the officers joined her and they kissed passionately."

"I can just visualize it. 'Tatania, your father, the Grand Duke, has granted me your hand. I am leaving tomorrow to join my regiment, the Fourteenth Dragoons. Be mine tonight!' "

"Oh, Ivan," Laura took me up, "I'm burning with love's fever. Promise you will marry me in Saint Petersburg!"

"Yes, Tatania, all the bells will ring, we shall flee to Kiev in a carriage, to the castle of my ancestors. You will be its mistress, you will reign over my people, my faithful mujiks. We'll go on long horseback rides in the steppes and I'll buy you a carriage like Doctor Zhivago's."

"Yes, a carriage with heavy furs and tiny bells. We'll drink vodka and eat caviar and . . ."

Behind us, someone coughed. I turned around. It was an ancient usherette with a gray bun at the back of her head.

"Excuse me, but the third act has just begun."

The foyer was empty, there was no one but us. Through the padded doors we could hear the queen declaiming. She seemed as angry as ever. Evidently nothing had changed since the preceding act.

"Should we go back in?"

Laura didn't seem very enthusiastic. "If you want to, but I'd rather leave."

We left. The empty corridors reeked of expensive dust. Behind the checkroom counter; two little old ladies were knitting away at full tilt.

Outside it was lovely: neon lights illuminated the chestnut trees. We strolled down the boulevard like a couple of Parisian old-timers.

"Should we go home or do you want to walk a little more?"

"Let's go as far as the square and back."

As we sauntered along, I noticed something we'd never discussed: the gradually formed habit of walking quite close together. For example, before stepping up or down a curb, I slow down without even being aware of it. My leg right next to hers, we move together without changing our pace.

In front of Wepler's, florists' booths were still open. Amid bunches of carnations and roses, their stems immersed in water-filled tin cylinders, a sign proclaimed: TOMORROW, JULY 25—SAINT JACQUES' DAY.

My name day. It was a coincidence, but what gave me a jolt was the fact that we had left Menton a full three weeks ago, that for three weeks we'd been living together. For a moment it seemed unbelievable; I would have sworn we'd been gone no more than a week.

"Do you know what day this is?"

"Yes, Friday."

"No, the date, do you know the date?"

"The twenty-fourth."

My second surprise. Unlike me, she had not lost contact with reality, and I couldn't refrain from pointing it out to her. "I was so sure that your mad passion for me had made you lose count of the days."

She didn't answer immediately. We continued to walk, passing lighted shop windows. Then abruptly she said: "I didn't lose count. I know it's the twenty-fourth because on the thirty-first I have to be in New York."

You often read in books that when a man suffers a shock, whether physical or mental, "everything begins to spin around," or "he held on to the wall to avoid falling," or even "suddenly everything was plunged into darkness." Well, for me, it wasn't at all like that. The statue on the Place de Clichy didn't budge an inch, I continued to walk straight ahead and the street lamps lost none of their power.

A bus passed, brilliantly lighted, and teenagers on motorcycles, their wheels scraping the curb, whizzed by. Everything remained exactly the same. Only one thing had changed: the future. In seven days Laura would no longer be here. That was all.

Of course she had her own life, her friends, her work. Everything wasn't going to come to a standstill just because she had met me. Although blind, she was still young, pretty, intelligent, and there were millions of men in the world. When you stopped to think, what actually had happened during these three weeks? We had had a marvelous time, we'd made love, we'd traveled a little, not much . . . We'd helped each other to spend a vacation that started out like any other and we'd turned it into a good thing, a gay interlude, but maybe that wasn't enough. For her, life hadn't begun the day she met me in a Menton movie theater.

"You haven't said anything . . ."

One day she had impressed upon me the difficulty of lying to a blind person. So why try? Anyway, I had no wish to.

"I was thinking of your going away. Why didn't you mention it before?"

"I didn't see any point. When you start counting the days, you don't live as well. I didn't want you to wake up each morning thinking, fourteen more days, only another week . . ."

I cleared my throat. "How will you get to America?"

"I'm not planning to swim there. Edith and I are going together. Our plane tickets have been reserved. I've been asked to take part in the administration of a psychological institute and I'm also supposed to teach a few courses at a university there."

"And . . . will it be interesting?"

"I have no idea. That's the whole point of my going there, to see for myself and then decide. I don't have to accept, and anyway, I won't be staying there forever."

"No, of course not."

She stopped suddenly and pointed straight ahead, toward the Place Blanche. "Listen."

The sounds were distant but quite clear: rumblings, horns blowing, a mixture of shouts and music.

Closer to us a song broke out:

> *Aime-moi, aime-moi*
> *Quand je suis dans tes bras*
> *Je dis: oh! la la la la la la. . . .*

Laura smiled. Perhaps for the first time since I'd known her it wasn't a real smile.

"It's some sort of fair," she said.

I too made an effort to sound lighthearted. "Do you want to go? I have some change in my pocket."

"Let's!"

We plunged into the crowd, the air reeking of waffles, imitation nougat, and caramel. Husky fellows were sauntering about, their hands in their revolver pockets, stomachs thrust forward, shirts open to their waists. People were milling about in front of the "Thousand and One Nights": three girls with padded bras and spangled skirts were swaying their hips against a backdrop of painted canvas with plywood palm trees. Nearby was the booth for wrestlers. Laura wanted to stop and listen to their patter. Three men were on the platform. One, skinny and nervous, was doing some shadow-boxing and jumping around frantically. A big, flabby, lethargic fellow wearing a leopard skin was named "The Strangler." And the third was a burly chap in red tights and hood with a black bat across his chest.

"And here, ladies and gentlemen, is someone whose

face nobody can bear to look at, who has never been
beaten in the thousand matches he's fought on the two
hemispheres. I ask anyone who might be tempted to
challenge him to think twice before coming into the ring.
The Vampire of Düsseldorf, that's his name, makes mincemeat of all his opponents, whether it be wrestling, English
or French boxing, karate, close-combat fighting, judo,
jujitsu. If you're hesitating, you may prefer "The Battling
Kid," lightweight champion of Tunis, a terrific puncher.
Or else "The Strangler," a powerful brute whose savagery
is beyond compare. With his bare hands he can twist an
iron bar five inches in diameter!"

Laura leaned toward me. "How about giving that
deadly haymaker of yours a try?"

It was difficult to get away from the crowd. Our ears
rang from the noise of the shooting gallery.

"It's funny, at the lottery you still win the same dolls
they used to hand out ages ago—with big hats and long
blue dresses."

"Yes," Laura replied. "Some things from the time
when we were young never change, and lottery dolls are
one of them. That's better than nothing . . ."

I couldn't head the rest of what she said because of the
racket coming from the "Russian Mountains" and the
noise of the loudspeaker, to say nothing of the women's
cries and the children's shouts as they rushed up and
down the mounds of fake snow.

Nearby were the miniature crash cars. The din was
deafening.

"Would you like some peanuts?" I had spotted a vendor
off to one side, between the "Phantom Train" and
Madame Amilcar, the fortune-teller. She had all sorts of
diplomas and specialized in affairs of the heart. She read
Tarot cards, palms or tea leaves.

I bought some peanuts for Laura and a roll of licorice
for myself. In the center of the sweet black spiral was a

little pink sugar pearl, another thing that hadn't changed.

Laura was fumbling inside her bag, her arm over mine. "We're so frivolous," she said. "Instead of attending that play at the theater, we go and eat peanuts in Montmartre."

I was chewing on my licorice, enjoying every mouthful. As we came to Professor O'Brien's wild animals (lions from Tanganyika, gorillas from the equatorial forest, crocodiles from the Amazon, tigers from Bengal), I decided to make a stab at it.

"How would you feel about getting married?"

The peanut, which she had shelled, was gently rolling about in her hand. She tossed it up to my mouth, and I caught it between my teeth. Laura leaned her head on my shoulder and we walked off like that, amid the blare of horns, the crack of rifle shots, the shouts and the songs.

Only seven days left.

# Lazybones

JULY twenty-seventh.

In two days she'll be gone, leaving by plane for Nice. I'll take her to the airport, Edith will meet her at the other end. Everything has been neatly arranged like a score for sad music.

Last night we had guests—Simon and Lydia. They were delighted to come. Lydia is a homebody, but very lively. She was born blind but didn't realize her condition until she was eight years old. It both surprised and amused her. For a long time, so she told us, she just laughed about it.

I did the cooking under Laura's strict supervision. My one worry was that the cake wouldn't rise, but it finally did. The rest was a great success.

Simon is very gentle and kind. I got along well with him. We discussed literature at length and I found him extremely knowledgeable. To my surprise, I was completely at home with both of them and felt neither pity nor condescension.

When Simon and I were alone for a few minutes, he seemed to want to talk about Laura. Evidently, he took a friendly interest and was concerned about us as a couple. There's so much goodness in that man that I felt myself the afflicted one. But Laura and Lydia soon joined us and, to my regret, the conversation changed. I thought that if ever Laura and I decide to live together or get married, Simon is the person I would go to for advice. He must know a good deal about the world of the blind that's unfamiliar to me. Among other things, he might be able to tell me whether it would be possible for Laura and me to continue together. One month isn't a lifetime. We've managed to be extremely happy for twenty-three days—maybe that's all you can expect, maybe I shouldn't hope for more. But perhaps he could teach me how to preserve our fragile happiness, how to avoid the clumsy mistakes of a sighted person.

As we drank our coffee the conversation turned to Maxime and at once I sensed an obvious uneasiness. No one had had any news of him for quite some time, but that wasn't surprising. Occasionally months went by without any sign of life from him. Then, one fine day, for no apparent reason, he would resurface, only to disappear once again.

As I listened, I had the distinct impression that Maxime was not really one of them, that they were leery of his volatile moods, his enigmatic behavior. They seemed to sense, with a keenness far greater than mine, an element of drama in his personality.

"Sometimes," Simon remarked, "an afflicted person makes the mistake of using his handicap as an instrument of power, as if he were touched by grace. I have the feeling now and then that Maxime is trying to raise blindness to the level of a religion. In ancient Egypt and Greece, the wise man, whose lot was superior to that of common mortals, was deaf, dumb and blind to worldly things. Perhaps this is what Maxime is attempting to do, in a different way."

I merely observed that the line between madness and

sanity was extremely thin. Then we talked about other things.

Laura mentioned her forthcoming trip to the United States but said nothing about planning to settle down there for a while.

I took both of them home and walked back. On my way I was thinking that we hadn't made love for four days and I missed it. Maybe I'm not so old after all.


"Turn around and admire me."

I swung around in my chair. She was standing in the center of the living room. The window was reflected in her dark glasses but it looked small and distorted. She held a white cane in her right hand. Somewhat shaken, I remained silent. Never having seen her with that gear, I was at a loss for words but I knew I had to say something.

"I didn't realize that you had the complete outfit . . ."

She laughed. "Edith thinks I should buy a seeing-eye dog, but I wouldn't know where to put it."

I took the cane—I had forgotten she even owned one. "Do you ever use it?"

"When I go out alone, but that's not often. I used it more three years ago. Miniskirts were the rage then and I wore them. One day on the Boulevard Haussmann I heard a woman say: 'A blind person ought to dress decently.' When I carry a cane I feel I must behave accordingly . . . It's hard to explain. People expect you to be serious and a little sad, and if you're not, they're shocked. They think a blind person who laughs is a fake."

For a moment I wondered why she was displaying herself to me with dark glasses and white cane, the insignia of her condition. Perhaps she wanted to convince me, although I already knew it, that she was first and foremost a cripple, that being a woman, being Laura

Bérien, was less important than the fact that she was blind.

We hadn't mentioned America or marriage again. These last days had passed quickly, too quickly.

She ran her fingers along my arm and cheek. "Ten-thirty in the morning and you're still unshaven and in pajamas . . . You're a lazybones, Bernier, a shiftless fellow."

Taking her in my arms, I held her tight with all my strength. I felt her lips on my forehead, my eyelids. Then suddenly she broke down.

As though a taut canvas had suddenly been rent by a knife, the sobs began. Doubled up on the carpet, Laura was simply a woman reduced to tears, and I didn't know how to comfort her, how to stem this sudden desolate outpouring.

"Laura, please . . . Take hold of yourself! What on earth is the matter?"

Gradually she quieted, her body shaken from time to time by long shudders, like the last tremors of an earthquake.

I knelt down. With her head in the crook of my arm, speaking softly, she said: "Pay no attention to me. I do this from time to time."

I disengaged myself, lit a cigarette and came back. She was still lying on the floor, her face turned toward the ceiling.

"Would you like a puff?"

She didn't answer but inhaled the warm blue smoke, and her eyes seemed to be following the wisps as they rose in the air.

"What's making you so unhappy?"

At first I thought she hadn't heard me, but when she answered I knew by the tone of her voice that she was about to say something that would be important for both of us.

"Don't think it's easy to be blind. Until now I've been gay, we've had a good time together, but I wouldn't want you to get the idea that it's easy or that I'm always so lighthearted. I try very hard to give you the feeling that I take my affliction lightly, as if it doesn't matter, something unimportant that can be overcome. Well, there's one thing I must tell you, Jacques: you can never overcome this kind of thing, do you hear? *Never!*"

She shouted the last word. Feeling terribly upset and utterly useless, I stood there, my arms dangling. What can I do, Laura? I can do nothing for you, there's simply nothing I can do.

Her voice was breaking now: "I work, I play around with you, I make love, I laugh, but there's one thing I never forget for a second, not for a single second: four years ago . . . I still had my sight."

Through the open door I saw myself in the hall mirror. My face was as white as the walls. For a minute I wondered: had the whole thing been an illusion from the very beginning, an enormous lie? Had she been play-acting when she laughed? Had she merely pretended to love me, pretended to be happy, pretended everything?

"The other night you asked me to marry you," she went on. "The least I can do is to be frank, to warn you that Laura Bérien is not a carefree girl who happens to be blind but doesn't give a damn. There's no such thing as a blind person who doesn't mind being blind."

"But . . ."

"Let me finish. Laura Bérien is a girl who's consumed with rage and grief. She may seem to have gotten over it, at least part of the time. But you've got to understand one thing, Jacques: people like me simply can't keep on an even keel for long. Any little thing can throw me off balance. You remember the second time I went into the water at Ostende? The weather was beautiful and I was so happy, and you must have been delighted to see me cavorting on the beach—well, at that very moment I was tempted to swim out to the open sea and just drown. Yet I love you and I was feeling good, the sun was wonderful, the water delightful—but in spite of all that . . ."

She lowered her head, probably unable to put into words the monstrous burden that separated her from the rest of the world.

"Maxime has thought about all this more than most of us and he feels he's found the answer: never try to share life with a sighted person. Having accepted the gulf that separates us, he's withdrawn to his dark corner and cut himself off from everyone who lives in the light. He behaves as if he belongs to a different species—he'll have nothing more to do with any of them. For a long time I considered his attitude excessive, but now and then I wonder: maybe he's right and all the others like Simon are wrong."

I reached for another cigarette. My index finger, yellow with nicotine, was trembling. I really should try to cut down.

She sat in silence for a while, rocking back and forth her chin on her knees, her arms around her legs, her face still streaked by tears.

Finally she asked. "Why don't you say something?"

"Because once you start talking, it's hard to ge a word in edgewise."

The beginning of a smile formed on her lips. A good sign.

"The next time," I added, "I'm going to demand equal time."

"Go ahead, I promise not to interrupt."

At this point I panicked. We had been in the habit of joking, of making light of everything. Now, all of a sudden, we'd have to talk, and talk seriously. The smoke made me cough but I finally found my voice.

"Believe it or not, I never doubted for a minute that

being blind is no joke. I'm over eighteen, I'm of age, you know. We've spent almost a month together and I honestly believed we could go on. I suggested marriage only because I'm a bit of a traditionalist, but if you object, that's perfectly all right. Anyway, I'd have to buy a new suit, invite the school principal—a whole lot of boring things like that . . . So if you'd rather, we could continue as we've been doing, here, or in my apartment, or anywhere you say. But there's one thing I do want to make clear: I don't know if it's possible for a sighted person and a blind one to be really happy together. I don't know and what's more I don't give a damn. What I do know is that Laura Bérien and Jacques Bernier can be happy."

Laura sighed. "Do you really feel you're cut out to be a nursemaid for the rest of your life?"

"You've told me what's on your mind, don't try to analyze mine, for God's sake!" I was shouting.

"Stop yelling. The lady downstairs will complain."

You aren't going to stop me this time, Laura. I've started and I'm going to say everything I have on my mind. I knelt in front of her, took her face in my hands, and talked for a long time. There I was, in my crumpled pajamas, unshaven, with a fiftieth birthday looming, and a paunch on the way. And Laura, all messy, hair a fright, in that old pair of slacks and her Shetland sweater. Yes, we were really a couple of Joes, as Anne would put it, an ideal duo for a magazine cover. Bérien-Bernier, number one on the summer hit parade, getting the grand prize for complicated love affairs . . . So I gave her a long lecture, like the principal on graduation day, and the sound of my voice soothed her.

" . . . and besides, I'm getting old. I'm fed up with living alone, eating scrambled eggs and washing a week's dirty dishes. If I asked you to marry me it's because you're what I want. It's as simple as that. I want to marry you. Don't try to read anything more into it. If you say yes, I'll be happy, if you say no—well . . . well, then screw it!"

She laughed softly and with tenderness. "You won't jump into the Seine?"

I laughed too and raised my right hand. "I swear."

She daydreamed for a minute, then put her hand on my arm. "There's so little time before I leave . . ."

My watch said twelve-thirty. Tomorrow at this time we'd be heading for the airport. I kissed her, loud country kisses, a smack on each cheek.

"We've got twenty-four hours, Laura. An eternity."

# Tanagra

*I* had a hard time making it out. The man with the cap who stood just in front of me blocked the view. I couldn't see them coming around the turn.

Oh, there they were! Just behind the hedge. Their caps glistened in the sun.

Laura's fingers dug into my arm. "Well, what's happening?"

"They're all bunched, no one's out in front . . . wait, yes, there they go, one's forging ahead, two behind, it's him, he's still in the race. God! If I only had field glasses!"

They were coming up fast, the sound of their pounding hooves neared, the necks of the three pacesetters stretching in unison.

Laura was jumping up and down. "Do you see our horse?"

Just then I saw him, the jockey crouching, his rump higher than his head, using his whip for all it was worth.

"He's third, he's catching up . . . he's about to pass, there he goes! He's out in front!"

Clumps of turf flew up and the ground trembled as they raced by.

"Is he winning?" Laura yelled.

I leaned over as far as I could. "Yes, he's made it, he's made it! He's the winner!"

I grabbed her. She smiled beatifically as the horses continued running in the distance. We wouldn't collect a fortune, but still it's a pleasant feeling . . .

The man with the cap turned around to face me. "Don't get so excited. They've still got another lap to go."

What a letdown! Laura's mouth fell open. "Do you think number six has a chance?"

The man looked at her, then at me. Amused surprise was in his voice and eyes. "You bet on number six?"

"Yes, why?"

"Because that nag is the king of the rubbish heap. What made you choose him?"

No use trying to impress him. He looked as if he was born in a paddock at Vincennes and would die queuing up before the ticket windows at Maisons-Lafitte. With all the deference that an amateur owes a professional, I confessed, "We've been betting on number six in every race."

He shook his head in pity. "You come to the races often?"

Contrite, Laura admitted: "No, this is the first time."

I was standing on my toes. "Look out! Here they come."

Without a word, the man in the cap handed me his binoculars. I adjusted them and suddenly a horse's nostril practically hit me in the eye. When I tried to get a clearer view, everything began to look murky. These field glasses are the devil.

"Well?" Laura asked. "What's that nag doing?"

There, I finally managed to set the lenses properly. The horses were again approaching but seemed to be slowing down. Where was that damn number six? I glanced over the field but couldn't spot him. Five was leading, followed by fourteen, then three, two and eight.

Good heavens, it wasn't possible! There he was, way over there, opposite the grandstand, a broken-down nag, the jockey still egging him on as if he were astride a sinking raft. I recognized the apple-green cap. It was him, all right.

I handed back the binoculars. "He's at least half a lap behind," I told Laura. "I've never seen such a nag. He looks as if he's running backward."

Disconsolately, she tore up our tickets, muttering: "He started off too fast. He wore himself out."

The race track regular chortled. "Even if he'd started off at a slow trot, he be dead on arrival. That horse has never won anything. It's not his fault, he has asthma. He's got good muscles, he's built for speed, he's got a fine pedigree, but he's got a terrible case of asthma. Any jockey will tell you that. When he wheezes at Auteuil you can hear him at Chantilly."

Laura laughed. "The one time we play the horses we pick a nag that has asthma. Can you give us a tip for the next race?"

I protested vehemently. "Oh, no! Let's quit. We haven't any luck. You saw for yourself . . ."

"You can do as you please," said the man. "I have no personal interest in it, but number seven is going to run away with this one."

"Thank you," said Laura.

The race was over. Laura looked at me pleadingly. "Just one more bet?"

I took her over toward the ticket windows and scolded her sternly: "I knew you'd drag me down to ruin. You're a compulsive gambler and you won't stop until I'm reduced to thievery or murder to pay off your outrageous debts. You're nothing but a gold digger! How many men have committed suicide because you brought them to the verge of bankruptcy?"

"Just one last fling on number seven. You heard what the man said."

"Don't try to get around me. But I'll buy you a beer, it's so hot."

Very few people were at the refreshment bar. The lawn was littered with the shreds of torn tickets. I settled Laura in front of a glass of beer and went to place a bet on number seven in the fourth race, eight in the fifth and nine in the sixth—just to hedge.

The beer was ice cold and foamy and the spot we were in very comfortable. The rest of the place was bustling with activity; hordes of people were rushing to the ticket windows. Laura eavesdropped, trying to catch numbers or names of horses.

"Have you got the line-up for the next race?"

I pulled the program from my pocket. "Yes. Why?"

"What's the name of number seven?"

"Cromagnon the Second."

She made a face. "A prehistoric horse! That's all we need. With a name like that, he'll never win."

"Well, it's a tough name for a horse to have, but that doesn't mean a thing. Do you want to wait here or go to the finish line?"

"It's nice here. Let's stay."

It was very nice. The weather was beautiful, the air smelled of the countryside, and it was only four o'clock. But I shouldn't have been looking at my watch.

It was funny how we happened to come here. She felt like going to the country where things were green, but it isn't easy from Paris. I suggested the Bois de Vincennes. But when we drove past the race track, we decided to come here instead.

Now the bell rang. The horses were at the post. I felt all tensed up.

"Tell me a story," Laura said, "any kind of story, to take my mind off those damned horses."

Frantically, I racked my brain. In the school lunchroom some of the teachers were always telling jokes but I never could remember a single one. But yes, there was one . . .

"Here's a riddle: my first is a body of water; my second is what a man says when he finds he's lost his change, and my . . ."

"Comédie Française! Good lord, I heard that one from a teacher when I was still in the lower form!"

I was miffed. "If you know so much, there's no point in my even trying. Wait here, I'm going to see what I can find out."

I didn't have far to go. Over the loudspeaker came the announcement. The winner was number twelve.

Laura was very disappointed. "Okay. Let's go. This isn't our lucky day."

That wouldn't do. I had to admit sheepishly, "I've already bet on the next two races. Let's stay until they're over."

That really surprised her. "You unspeakable louse! And you accuse me of being a compulsive gambler! Which ones?"

I looked at the program again. "Belle Fontaine and Tanagra."

Her face lit up. "Well, that's different. One of them is bound to win. I feel it in my bones."


A slow foxtrot.

Subdued lights, liquid tones from the piano, the guy at the drums was stroking his kettledrums with metal brushes. The musicians were dressed in light blue silken jackets that looked white in the spotlight.

We hadn't danced very much, only the slow fox trots, because that's all I know. Everything else has always seemed impossibly complicated, yet I admire people who leap out on the floor when they hear rock music or a rumba, as though it's the most natural thing in the world.

We were still shaken up by our big thrill that afternoon. Tanagra had won. "Hands down," as Laura said.

In any case, we'd decided to spend all our winnings tonight, which explained this sumptuous night club, the champagne and the fox trots. It was in a small street behind the Champs Elysées. There were only a few people, just some Americans and a couple eating oysters by the dozen and speaking in Périgord accents.

We were treated to some kind of strip tease by a Eurasian so heavily made up she didn't dare smile. After scattering all her clothing around the floor, she danced naked, juggling transparent baloons. There were a couple of other acts, including a singer with bad adenoids who tried to imitate Frank Sinatra. Every now and then the maître d'hôtel came over to see how we were getting on.

"Are Monsieur and Madame satisfied?"

"Everything's perfect, thank you."

He rather resembled a more worldly version of old Émile, the sauerkraut and Ricard man of our past. It seemed long ago, far away in another world—the beginning of our affair. Now we were nearing the end.

The fox trot was over and I led Laura back to our table. I had to keep looking at her, I wanted to remember her face forever. One thought kept plaguing me, even though I shut every door to keep it out: tomorrow I won't see her any more.

"Some champagne?"

"Please."

Silence gradually settled over us. Come, I might as well face it, this was just a brief reprieve, part of her was no longer with me.

Only the pianist was playing. I knew the tune, an American song that was popular a few years ago, but now sounding outmoded, as if the notes had gradually worn away. Perhaps music, like old stones, acquires a patina of sorts . . . The refrain grew louder, then died away. The couple eating oysters were talking quietly. Laura sat dreaming, her chin on her hand.

This was probably a perfect place for the eve of her departure: an old-fashioned cabaret resounding with the love songs of bygone days. As she sipped her drink her hair caught the light, encircling her head with a faint golden halo.

She was very beautiful tonight. It would have been hard to describe her. Anyway, why try? She was simply Laura, and she was going away.

Two guitars joined the piano. Not a slow fox trot but something I could manage. "May I have this dance, lovely lady?"

She smiled and stood up. We glided along the dance floor. Above us a spangled ball revolved, throwing out colored lights like specks of confetti.

"Dance closer to me."

It's true, I've always tended to hold my partner as if an imaginary barrier separated us. That's my 1930 personality, very proper and old fashioned.

I could feel her warmth and her perfume. No it wasn't possible, this couldn't be the end for us!

She raised her head as if she sensed that I was about to speak.

Her voice was low and a little husky. "I don't think I'll stay in New York," was all she said.

Very few people were on the floor, there was lots of space and an incredible thing happened: I, who didn't know how, who'd never learned to dance, well, I actually began to waltz! In my fervor I whirled her around and around. At least fifteen times we gloriously circled the floor. The flabby orchestra was still playing its rhythm for convalescents, but I didn't give a damn, I had my own music inside of me, all the waltzes—Strauss, Vienna, all of Austria and its drawing rooms—everything illuminated and glittering, and Laura twirling, her head bent back and laughing. I got a fleeting glimpse of the musicians and waiters. They looked as if they'd seen it all before. We finally stopped, unsteady with dizziness and champagne . . . I sank into my chair, my heart ready to burst.

Our last day, but who knows, maybe our luckiest. Tanagra had won and Laura would come back.

# Orly

*ALL passengers going to . . . passengers . . . to Teheran . . . going . . . flight 327 to Teheran, Air France, on flight . . . please go to . . . Air France flight 327 . . . gate number . . . now boarding . . .*

The voice reechoed as if bouncing off mountain walls.

I pulled Laura back to make room for a truckload of luggage. Years ago the stations were filled with the metallic noise of clanging motorcarts. Here, the wheels were cushioned with rubber and the driver pressed a soft bell to warn the travelers, then silently went on his way.

Mounds of trunks and suitcases rushed passed me and I glimpsed the labels—Hotels Plaza, Ritz, Excelsior, Georges V . . . London, Madrid, Valparaiso, Paris, New York . . . The world of de luxe travel was everywhere much the same, the rich going to the same expensive hotels, whether in Paris, Calcutta, or Los Angeles. The landscapes changed very little for them; soon they wouldn't bother to move.

"Wait for me here. I'll have your ticket checked."

I, who am always at a loss when it comes to formalities, immediately found the right ticket office. Very few people were traveling on Air-Inter. The woman in charge wore a chocolate-colored cap like a bellboy's. Her long purple nails slid down the list of passengers leaving for Nice.

"Laura Bérien . . ."

She tore off a coupon and handed me two cards, giving me instructions about where to turn them in. Before she could finish I managed to interrupt her.

"Laura Bérien is blind, would it be possible to . . ."

Without a second's hesitation, the expression on her face completely unaltered, she said: "Don't worry, she'll be looked after by the flight stewardess who will attend to her needs during the entire trip, from takeoff to arrival. I myself will notify the proper authorities."

Listening to her, I got the impression that Air-Inter served blind people exclusively, that nothing unusual was involved. She had already placed a banana-shaped telephone against her ear.

"Hello, a blind woman on flight two-fourteen. Yes, to Nice . . . Laura Bérien . . . Thank you." Click. She hung up.

So! That was that. Everything taken care of. The efficient clerk looked at me as if to say, why do you keep standing there?

I went to join Laura. There was an hour left, almost an hour.

She smiled when I put my hand on her knee. "Everything attended to?"

"Yes."

We were silent. Behind the glassed-in enclosures you could see the runways. A DC-8, glistening in the sun, began to move, then turned, its nose facing the hangers. Laura was wearing the ring I had given her. Her fingers toyed with the frames of her dark glasses.

I didn't know what to say and I knew she didn't either, yet the silence was hard to bear.

"Jacques?"

"Yes?"

"What will you do during the rest of your vacation?"

That was a good question. I hadn't thought about it. Another month to go, all of August, scorching hot and endless. I couldn't go back to Menton, walk down its streets, gaze at the Casino, look at the closed shutters of the Villa Caprizzi, wander about on an endless pilgrimage. No. Besides, I'm too lazy to take that long drive on the autoroute again, to say nothing of my battery, which is surely about to give out.

"I don't know . . . I think I'll stay in Paris for a while. It's not bad in August, it's quiet and deserted. I'll take long strolls, look in at some of the museums like an old prof who wants to improve his mind. I'll go and see Simon, that will please him."

I sensed that she was tense, tense and sad.

"I'm afraid you'll be bored all alone. Why don't you go and see Anne? Or else take a trip somewhere, that would be good for you."

"I feel fine. I'll take it easy and wander around. There's nothing so awful about just staying here."

She lowered her head, her fingers constantly fooling with her glasses.

"I don't like the idea of leaving," she said.

A little over half an hour left. Thirty-three minutes, to be precise.

"I've seen lots of movies where a girl like you is about to board a plane. The guy remains on the waiting-room bench, desolate, then slowly walks toward the car, his shoulders sagging. You see the girl hand in her ticket at the gate and enter the plane that's about to take her to the ends of the earth. Suddenly she turns, begins to run in the opposite direction, pushing people aside, knocking over piles of luggage, and arrives just as he's about to turn on the ignition, looking as if his life were over. She opens the door and throws herself at him passionately. The last scene is a car moving off, he's driving with one hand, a blissful look on his face. Her head's on his shoulder, her eyes are closed and tears of happiness flow unchecked down her cheeks. At this point, all the violins go into action."

She laughed. "Was that the picture where the girl who was blind at the beginning regains her sight?"

"Yes, the same one. You'll end up by thinking I can only remember idiotic movies."

Why hadn't I asked her to stay? It shouldn't have been difficult to tell her I was tired of hearing about her silly trip to New York, that I loved her and didn't want to suffer. But I've never been inclined to impose my will on others and I wasn't about to begin with her. Maybe I should have. Maybe I should have been firm and more candid. I ought not to have pretended to be the broad-minded man who of course understood her wanting to leave because of her work, who say it was a chance in a lifetime, and all that nonsense. Good lord, if I hadn't been so weak, we wouldn't be at Orly right now with this silence between us, as heavy and oppressive as the morning before a storm. I swallowed.

"Are you planning to write me?"

She nodded vigorously. "Of course."

"Naturally, I'll reply. But there's a problem. You can guess what it is."

Her fingers reached out and touched my face. "Edith will read me your letters, but I have nothing to hide from her. Even if you feel like sending me very erotic letters, pages and pages of them, go right ahead."

"Okay. I'll add a nice word for Edith at the end."

"I'm sure that will please her."

Another twenty minutes.

A Hindu family had taken the row of seats opposite us. One of the children was swinging his leg back and forth rhythmically, as if marking the seconds. He looked at us with eyes the exact color of the roasted chestnuts you buy in winter in front of the Montparnasse station.

"If . . . if you do come back, when do you think that will be?"

"The full training period, if I stay for it, usually lasts three months."

August . . . September . . . October . . . She could be back by the first of November. Late autumn is usually a beautiful time of year in Paris. On weekends I'll take her to the forests, to inns with high-beamed ceilings. There are so many things we haven't done!

That kid annoys me, now he's kicking the seat as if he were a metronome. God, so little time left! This is the moment when I ought to be thinking of something to say, something memorable, the kind of words great men utter at crucial moments. But I felt dry and empty.

Laura jumped up. "I haven't a single cigarette."

I searched my pockets. Three Gauloises, not enough.

"Don't move. I'll go get you some."

"No, let me come with you."

And what if she herself didn't want to leave? What if she couldn't bear the thought of parting from me? Why should she want to go with me to buy the cigarettes? Barely ten minutes left.

There were crowds of people, including a boisterous group with duffel bags and pennants. Probably a soccer team, or something of the sort. I tried to protect her from the crowd.

"Two packages of Gauloises."

I stuffed a package in her jacket pocket. She opened it immediately and tore the paper the wrong way, which was very unlike her.

The bell announcing a departure rang over our heads and I felt my heart sinking. She clutched my sleeve and I took the cigarette she handed me.

I was looking for matches and not finding them when the loudspeaker called out: *All passengers on Air-Inter flight two-fourteen to Nice are requested to go to gate number seven.*

Well, there it was. The end of it all.

There was a hubbub, people were running. Things couldn't be happening so fast, it wasn't quite time. We returned to the waiting room. The child was still beating time with his feet, looking at us as if the span he was ticking off was ours.

I picked up her traveling bag and my fingers tensed on her shoulder.

"Let's not hurry," Laura said. "They always alert you much too soon."

I could feel the sweat running down my forehead. A drop reached my eyebrow and stopped there. Outside, on the other side of the windows, the sun was beating down unbearably.

"The fact is, Laura, I . . . well, I don't think I've told you often enough that I love you. I wouldn't want you to think I don't love you or that I don't love you very much. I'm going to be very lost without you. And I just can't get it through my head that you're really leaving."

Abruptly, as if suddenly dazzled by a powerful light, she put on her dark glasses. "I know. I can't quite realize it myself. Maybe the girl in your movie did the right thing . . ."

*All passengers for flight number two-fourteen . . .*

"Damn," Laura said, "it seems as if we're acting out the final scene of a five-act play."

As we talked, I took her arm. The gate numbers were over there, at the other end of the waiting room. The final moment had come.

"Laura Bérien?"

It was the airplane stewardess. She must have spotted us because of Laura's dark glasses and because I was holding her arm, or maybe something indefinable in the way she carried her head, the way she walked.

"That's me."

"I'm responsible for looking after you and seeing that you're comfortable. If you need anything at all, please don't hesitate to ask, I'll be quite near you all during the trip."

"Thank you."

The girl cast a rapid, inquisitive glance at me. "I'll come and get you in a few minutes. Please give me your ticket."

"Here it is. I won't budge."

The stewardess's heels clicked as she hurried away. We were alone, a little apart from the others, who crowded near the gate as if afraid they might miss the plane.

"Well, here we are!"

"Yes, here we are."

We laughed together. I'd never noticed until this minute how white her teeth were. There were also fine little wrinkles at the corners of her eyelids. I cleared my throat.

"I have the feeling that neither of us is very good at farewells."

A Boeing was warming up. It was still a distance away and the sun shone on its fuselage. The engines were making a good deal of noise. Perhaps this was the plane that would take her away.

"Are you going straight home?"

"No, first I'll check to make sure your plane is leaving. Then I'll wave my handkerchief until my arm drops."

I saw the stewardess coming back, walking briskly. "Here comes your bodyguard."

Laura handed me the stub of her cigarette. There was no ashtray in sight so I crushed it with my heel.

"I have one suggestion," she said. "We could kiss."

"That was my intention."

Her lips tasted fresh, like sugared raspberries.

The stewardess came up, smiled as they do in the ads,

and put her hand on Laura's suede jacket. All the other passengers were already piling into a small bus that waited below us.

"Goodbye, Laura."

With her free hand, she waved as the stewardess took her off. The girl was chatting, showering her with attention. But Laura didn't answer. They disappeared.

I saw no point in staying any longer. I didn't know which of the planes was hers and I wanted to spare myself the absurdity of following one flight with fixed eyes when actually she might be on another.

It was wonderfully blue up there; the flight would not be troubled by bad weather. There was really nothing to fear except mechanical failure or a hijacking.

Forcing myself to turn around, I went back across the terminal. The child was still there opposite the chairs we had occupied. He was looking straight ahead of him, but now his legs were still.

In my pocket I came across the forgotten envelope that had been there since this morning. It was a letter from Anne. Strange that it should have arrived today, as if, with Laura gone, the past was returning. The adventure over, my daughter reappeared.

I suppose I'm an unnatural father. I hadn't read it yet, nor had I given her much thought during the past month. But now I had all the time in the world and didn't feel like going home. In fact, I hated to leave the airport because that would sever the last time with Laura.

I settled down on one of those imitation leather seats and unfolded the letter. It was quite long, yet Anne, who is so very talkative, does not enjoy writing. She was fine, had two television shows in prospect for after the vacation, Frédéric was as nice as ever and they were still in love.

It's been much warmer and the two of us are now

alone in the farmhouse. Max was the last of the gang
to leave. I think they all scared you when you first
arrived. I wondered if you had gone off with Laura
partly to escape from a group you'd found a bit too
rowdy, too different.

Anne's an idiot. I know her. When she says silly things
it's usually because she's worried. She must be very worried because this is about the silliest thing she's ever said.
Nothing in all the world could have stopped me from
going off with Laura; I would have turned my back on all
the luxuries of an oriental palace, all the charms of a
harem, all the delights of Arabia. To be perfectly candid,
Anne, I'm sure that even if you had asked me to stay,
I would have refused . . . even if you were still a little
girl and had begged me not to leave, I would have left
anyway.

There's never been anything in my life that would
make good copy for a novel, sweet Anne, not even anything, I suppose, that might add up to a real life. So I
had to make a stab at it . . .

I know you're a venerable professor, full of common
sense, logic and all that, and you may think I'm just
plain jealous. But that's not it at all. It's so much more
serious that I've hesitated all along to say anything.
Even if things seem easy for you today, I can't believe
they'd be easy tomorrow. I discussed this with a friend
who's a specialist in such matters—very discreetly, don't
worry—and he stated quite badly that living with a
handicapped person is difficult psychologically, hard on
the nerves. I'm afraid it would be hard on you. You
would suffer, foolishly, and it would bother me to know
that you're sad when we meet over our steaming couscous on the Rue de Bièvre.

Because of Laura, it seemed I had almost completely
forgotten that I had another woman in my life. She's
been there for twenty-four years but it wasn't until today

that the fact was really brought home to me.

I've thought of all that, Anne, oftener than you, I'm sure, and I have two answers, but the first is enough: I love Laura.

There's a second, hidden, more selfish reason: my last chance, little Anne, my very last chance for love. I'm getting older . . . there won't be others, Laura's the last. After her, if she shouldn't return, there'll be nothing but exam papers, friends, longings, movies alone on Sundays, school graduations, then retirement some day. I'll play *belote* in the spring in the Luxembourg gardens and grow old alone, and I don't want to.

It's as simple as that.

In movies about aging gangsters, there's always one guy who pulls his last job. Well, I'm that gangster. Perhaps this is true for Laura too. Maybe we serve as crutches for one another in order to keep going. At school, when you were seventeen, you delighted in poems describing the first look, the first kiss, the first love . . . and you yourself wrote poems about it. So I'm asking, Anne, if first love still moves you, let me live my last love.

Frédéric keeps telling me that it's none of my business, and of course he's right. But he's also wrong, because anything that happens to you is also my business and I'd like to help but don't know just how. I'd like you to avoid making a bad mistake, to be happy. I know you're young, strong and handsome, but that's no reason why I shouldn't look after you. Years from now I'll take you to the Guignol theater on Thursdays. Meanwhile, I can only say to you, "Father, before you cross the street, look both ways."

Kisses,
Anne

Like a diamond bird, a plane silently glided past the window.

I will answer her tonight, a good long letter.

I rose from my seat. Laura's plane had left by now and suddenly I was afraid I wouldn't be able to recall her face. Like an idiot, I didn't ask her for a single photograph. Maybe it was just as well. Photos are the privilege of sighted people. We were both in the same boat now: we would see each other only with the eyes of memory until she returned.

Outside, the sun over the parking lot beat down murderously. The frame of the car was scorching. I opened the windows to air it out.

She'll come back. She said she would and I must believe her.

But perhaps her life there will blot out a good many things. A few weeks in America and Jacques Bernier, the little summer holiday teacher, will gradually fade away— or maybe quickly. Besides, she might find the work absorbing—new situations, greater responsibilities—such things might delay her return, or even prevent it forever . . .

As I started the car, a large Peugeot 404 shot out, then braked. The driver gestured his apology, smiled, and let me pass. That in itself was a miracle, the first time a member of that killer race had behaved like a human being. Emerging from the tunnel, I passed three trucks, honking my horn gaily. The light sparkled on my windshield, flooding the car. I turned on the radio full blast. The road ahead was clear.

Maybe all that didn't mean anything, but I was sure then, my love, my blind love, that you would come back.

# John Updike

| | | |
|---|---|---|
| ☐ THE CENTAUR (100) | 22922-X | 1.75 |
| ☐ COUPLES (50) | C2935 | 1.95 |
| ☐ A MONTH OF SUNDAYS (50) | C2701 | 1.95 |
| ☐ THE MUSIC SCHOOL (100) | 23279-4 | 1.75 |
| ☐ THE POORHOUSE FAIR (100) | 23314-6 | 1.50 |
| ☐ RABBIT REDUX (75) | 23247-6 | 1.95 |
| ☐ RABBIT, RUN (75) | 23182-8 | 1.75 |
| ☐ PIGEON FEATHERS (100) | Q749 | 1.50 |

# Joyce Carol Oates